PUFFIN BOOKS

MASTER OF THE GROVE

When his home is destroyed after an attack, Derin sets out to look for his missing father, captured by soldiers of the Citadel. But he is handicapped by his lameness and forced to use a crutch; his only companions on his quest are an old woman, Marna, and a raven which mysteriously attaches itself to him.

Derin's people, upland farmers, are caught up in a war between the people of the mountains, governed by the Sacred Circle of the Grove, and those of the plains, ruled by the Council of the Citadel. There should have been peace between them according to a formula devised by Wenborn the Wise. But Krob has seized power by murdering one of the ten members of the Circle, and with the aid of the magical staff of the Grove proceeds to unleash a terrible vengeance against the plains people.

The pace of this gripping fantasy never lets up until the final moment when Derin finds himself face to face with Krob, 'Master of the Grove', together with the mystery of his own identity.

Master of the Grove won the Australian Children's Book of the Year Award for 1983. It is the third of Victor Kelleher's fantasy novels for children—*Forbidden Paths of Thual* and *The Hunting of Shadroth* are also published in Puffin.

[illegible]

[illegible]

[illegible]

[illegible]

[illegible]

[illegible]

VICTOR KELLEHER

MASTER OF THE GROVE

PUFFIN BOOKS

Puffin Books, Penguin Books Ltd, Harmondsworth, Middlesex, England
Penguin Books, 40 West 23rd Street, New York, New York 10010, U.S.A.
Penguin Books Australia Ltd, Ringwood, Victoria, Australia
Penguin Books Canada Ltd, 2801 John Street, Markham, Ontario, Canada L3R 1B4
Penguin Books (N.Z.) Ltd, 182-190 Wairau Road, Auckland 10, New Zealand

First published by Kestrel Books 1982
Published in Puffin Books 1983
Reprinted 1983, 1984, 1985 (twice), 1987

Printed in Australia by
The Book Printer,
Maryborough, Victoria

Set in Ehrhardt

Contents

1 Awakening 7
2 The Witch People 20
3 A Shadow 30
4 Conflict 43
5 The Sword of the Kings 55
6 The Cave of Obin 67
7 The Thief 79
8 The Woodlands 91
9 Captive 103
10 Within the Citadel 117
11 The East 132
12 The Place of the Circle 148
13 Krob 160
14 Bearer of the Staff 176

1. Awakening

When he opened his eyes he could remember nothing, not even his own name. It was almost like waking up for the very first time, looking out through bewildered eyes upon a world he did not understand. Everything about the past - his own identity, where he had come from - was a total blank. He knew only that he was extremely cold and that his head ached unbearably. Groaning softly to himself, he rolled over and looked about him. It took him a moment or two to focus clearly; then he found that he was somewhere in a wood, lying stretched out near the edge of a deep bank of snow. There was no trace of colour in the scene before him: overhead, the sky was a dull, wintry grey; and the wood itself was etched starkly in black and white, the dark trunks of trees rising up out of a uniform blanket of snow.

He groaned once again as he struggled clumsily to his feet and stood leaning against a nearby branch. His head continued to throb steadily and he reached up as though to still the pain, only to discover that his forehead was swollen and caked with dried blood. It occurred to him that he might have been attacked and left there in the woods to die. But who would have done such a thing? And for what reason? He searched his mind for some shred of memory, for any clue that might help him recapture the past, but all he encountered was darkness and silence. Nothing. His mind, it seemed, was empty of all save the sensations of cold and pain.

The cold especially could not be ignored. Despite his thick woollen clothing his teeth were chattering uncontrollably, and he knew even in his present confused state that unless he found shelter soon he might well freeze to death. With that thought to urge him on, he took one faltering step forward; but the moment he placed his full weight upon his right foot, he collapsed back onto the soft powdery snow.

Puzzled, he sat up and felt his leg below the knee. The ankle-joint, to his dismay, was slack and loose. Yet it didn't seem to be broken, because it caused him no pain. Then why, he wondered, couldn't it bear his weight?

As if in answer to his own question, a vague picture drifted across his mind. It was the blurred image of a face, the eyes wide open, staring at him, though not unkindly. He tried to remember who it was, but the image had faded too quickly and he could not make it return.

With a shrug of the shoulders, he gave up the effort of trying to recall the past and struggled to his feet once more. Now, for the first time, he noticed that he was not simply stranded within a featureless winter landscape. A jumble of footprints led through the snow to where he now stood. Some of the footprints, he knew instinctively, were his own. And the others? There was something both peculiar and familiar about them - the regular star-patterned mark beside the footprints; the exact shape of the boots outlined in the snow - something he would have cause to remember later. For the present, he was merely aware that they were associated in some indirect way with the staring eyes he had glimpsed a few moments earlier.

He had no time to dwell on this strange connexion. A blast of cold wind moaned through the leafless trees, lifting the surface snow and making it swirl about his feet. Already, to judge from the uncertain light, it was late afternoon and he still had to find shelter from the bitter night ahead. Pulling his woollen collar up around his face and taking care not to put too much weight upon his lame foot, he hobbled slowly away, following the clear trail of footprints across the snow.

As he made his way through the wood, nursing his right foot, floundering and sometimes falling in the deep snow, he looked much smaller than he really was. Perhaps it was the effect of the gaunt trees which surrounded him or of the way he hunched himself up against the cold. For he was actually quite tall and sturdily built for a boy of fourteen. This only became apparent when he emerged from the woods about ten minutes later and stood up straight, surveying the open, rolling country which now stretched away before him.

This open farmland was also covered in a layer of deep snow which blotted out roads and hedges and robbed the scene of most of its detail. In the far distance he could just see what he took to be a village, wisps of wood-smoke rising lazily from a huddle of dwellings. But closer at hand what caught and held his attention were the burned-out remains of a farmhouse. It appeared desolate enough in the late afternoon light, with its cracked stone walls which had collapsed in several places and its fallen roof beams; and normally he would have avoided such a place. What attracted him now was the fact that the house had obviously been destroyed quite recently, perhaps earlier that day, for the charred remains of the roof beams were still smouldering. And at the thought of fire and warmth, he hurried down the slope as fast as his lame foot would allow.

The ruin was even more desolate at close quarters. It was clear that a struggle had taken place there, for several broken weapons littered the snow round about. But he took little notice of these signs, intent only on escaping from the deep chill which bit into him. Clambering hastily through the half-obstructed doorway, he crouched down in the thick layer of ash which covered the earth floor, allowing its lingering heat to rise up into him. Gradually his teeth stopped chattering and soon his hands and feet began to tingle back to life. With a sigh of pleasure he stood up - and only then noticed the figure watching him silently from the doorway.

She was an old woman with wild grey hair and she was draped in a long tattered cloak which reached almost to her feet.

'So you survived then, Derin,' she said in a low accusing voice. 'I might have guessed you would. What surprises me is your coming back here. I thought your sense of shame would have kept you clear of this place, after the way you acted.'

'You ... you know me?' he said falteringly.

'Know you!' she said with a mirthless laugh. 'Do you think a scratch like that on your forehead is enough to stop me recognizing you? Didn't I nurse you after your mother died? Haven't your father and I tried to make something of you these many years? Though much good it's done us. No, boy, you can't hide from me so easily.'

'But I'm not trying to hide from anyone!' he said desperately. 'All I want to know is who I am and what I'm doing here.'

Again she chuckled mirthlessly.

'Oh, you're Derin all right,' she said, shaking her head confidently. 'Always the crafty one. Never caught without an excuse.'

'Is that my name? Derin?' he asked eagerly. 'And you mentioned my father. Who is he? Where is he now?'

He spoke with such unfeigned sincerity that the old woman's eyes narrowed, and for the first time she looked at him less accusingly.

'I know your tricks,' she said, but without her former certainty. 'You can't fool me.'

'I'm not trying to fool anybody!' he burst out. 'I can't remember! Don't you see that? I've forgotten everything!'

He half turned away and put his hands up to his swollen, still aching forehead. He heard the old woman clamber through the doorway and come towards him; felt her coarse hands brush his own.

'This is no time for lies,' she said quietly; 'not after what's happened to us today.'

'I'm not lying to you,' he said wearily, 'I swear it.'

'Look at me, then. Surely you remember me.'

He turned towards her and looked into her calm grey eyes. Just for an instant a trace of recognition flickered somewhere at the back of his mind. It wasn't the face itself, old and stubborn, which he seemed to remember, or the wild bush of grey hair, but rather her eyes. It was as if he had looked into them once before, long ago.

'Yes,' he said hesitantly, 'perhaps . . . I'm not sure.'

'And what happened here today,' she asked, watching his reaction carefully, 'doesn't that come back to you?'

He shook his head.

'I remember nothing of it,' he replied.

Apparently satisfied, she picked her way through the ash and debris towards the doorway.

'But aren't you going to tell me?' he asked her.

'Time enough for explanations,' she replied grimly. 'A bad tale can always wait. First we must get some warm food in our bellies, and for that we need a fire. While the light's still good I'll collect some dry sticks.'

'All right,' he agreed, 'but let me do that for you.'

He began hobbling over towards her, but she held up her hand, indicating he should remain where he was.

'Don't play the hypocrite with me, boy,' she said, a faint expression of disbelief on her face. 'In all your life you've never lifted a hand to help anybody. Now isn't the time for pretence.'

Before he could reply, she walked quickly away up the slope, her stride firm and strong despite her age.

Left to himself for a short time, he pondered the scanty information he had gathered so far. Even the little that had been said suggested an image of himself that was less than pleasant. Crafty, she had called him, and lazy or selfish. And then, earlier, there had been some mention of his shame, whatever that meant.

Almost as confused as he had been before, he watched impatiently as she returned down the slope, dragging a log behind her and with a bundle of sticks slung over one shoulder. Without thinking, he rose to help, but again she waved him away.

'I can do this for myself,' she said shortly. 'I've had enough practice over the years.'

'That may be,' he said, strangely hurt by her attitude, 'but why won't you let me help you now?'

'Because tomorrow our ways part forever,' she answered, 'and when we turn our backs on each other, I don't want to be in your debt, not even over a trifle like carrying wood.'

'But why should we part?' he asked. 'Where is there to go?'

She shrugged.

'You can do as you please; stay here; go back and hide yourself in the woods; whatever you choose. I wash my hands of you. As for me, my road lies far beyond here.'

By way of explanation, she raised one arm vaguely in the direction of the south, allowing her hand to circle round towards the east. As she did so, her cloak fell open, revealing a thick full-skirted dress made from the wool of black sheep. At the unexpected sight of her dress, Derin heard himself say:

'But you can't leave here.'

'Why not?' she answered quickly.

To his own surprise, he felt he knew the answer to that question.

'Because ...' he began slowly, 'it is forbidden ... forbidden by ...'

'Go on,' she said tensely.

He made an enormous effort to complete what he had begun: '... the Witch People ...' he stuttered out, 'the Witch People are ...'

But the words refused to come. He shook his head.

'It's no good,' he said, giving up, 'it's gone again. You'll have to tell me, Marna.'

Her name seemed to slip out of his mouth before he was even aware he knew it. Through the gathering twilight he could see her watching him intently, her wrinkled face drawn into an expression he could not interpret.

'That knock on the head couldn't have been too hard,' she said dryly. 'I see that some things are coming back to you. I wonder how much more you can remember.'

At the time he couldn't be completely sure, but he had the impression that there was a note of strange anxiety in her voice as she spoke those words.

With the coming of night the wind had risen, and they were thankful enough to take refuge within the protective walls of the farmhouse. There Marna lit a small fire while Derin roamed around searching for food. All he managed to find were a few handfuls of oats scraped from the bottom of one of the stone bins which stood in the corner of what had once been the kitchen. Marna cooked these into a thick porridge, using an old iron pot she had discovered half-buried in the ash. It was not a very appetizing meal, unflavoured by salt or milk, but it did at least warm them and fill their bellies.

As he ate, spooning the lumpy mixture from the pot with a piece of stick, Derin looked questioningly about him. He knew that these rough stone walls, lit by the flickering light from the fire, should have appeared completely familiar to him. How often he must have sat in this self-same room in the company of his father. Yet now it was as if he were seeing it for the very first time.

He glanced over at Marna who had already eaten her fill and was leaning back against the crumbling remains of the chimney. She had, he realized, been watching him for some minutes and there was a half-smile on her old face.

'I thought at first you were lying to me,' she said. 'You can't blame me for that; it's what I've grown used to from you. But now I see you were speaking the truth. You really can't remember, can you?'

He shook his head.

'All right,' she conceded, 'I suppose I'll have to tell you about our life here - though as I warned you earlier, it isn't a pleasant tale.'

In the brief pause which followed, he wanted to spring to his own defence even before she had begun, to ask her how he could be sure she wasn't the one who was doing the lying. But he forced himself to remain silent, waiting to hear what she would say.

'I'd better go right back to the beginning,' she said thoughtfully, 'to when I first came here. Up until then I'd always lived alone, in a cottage next to the woods. I had no land and I survived by selling herbs and cures for sickness. It wasn't an easy life, and when I heard that your mother had died of pneumonia, during a bad winter, I offered myself as a nurse and housekeeper. You were a toddler then, not quite two, but already wilful and bent on having your own way. Forever whining and begging for attention, using that foot of yours as an excuse for ...'

'Do you mean I've always had a lame foot?' he broke in anxiously.

She nodded, apparently ignoring the expression of deep dismay on his face.

'Yes, you were born that way,' she went on. 'That's one thing I didn't think you'd forget. You certainly never let us forget about it. Any other child would have made the best of things, but not you. You used that one small affliction as an excuse for doing nothing, expecting to be waited on from morning till night; never ...'

But once again he interrupted her.

'Yes,' he said abruptly, feeling not only disappointed, but also shamed and repelled by this unpleasant image of himself, 'you've made all that plain enough. What I want to find out about is my father - who he is and what he does.'

'That's easily told,' she said. 'Your father's name is Ardelan. He farms this narrow tract of land which stretches from the woods to the road further down the slope. He's never been rich, but neither has he been poor. Always, even in the worst seasons, he's managed to produce enough to support himself. That's why, when the trouble began, he was able to keep out of things. For a time, anyway.'

'Trouble?' he asked quickly. 'What kind of trouble?'

She raised both hands in a vague gesture.

'Who knows? There's plenty of talk around the place, but in a remote area like this no one can be certain.'

'And this trouble, whatever it is, arrived here earlier today?'

'Yes,' she said, running one hand through her wild grey hair. 'The soldiers of the Citadel came this morning, soon after dawn. I was all for keeping the peace, but your father is a stubborn, strong-minded man. And so, as you probably guessed, there was a fight. A fierce one while it lasted.'

'You mean my father is dead?' he asked, unable to keep the alarm out of his voice.

'Oh no,' she said reassuringly. 'He's been taken captive, but otherwise he's alive and well. You see, the soldiers didn't just want supplies - cattle and sheep and such like - they also wanted men to swell their own ranks. Your father is now on his way to the plains. Like most of the able-bodied men around here, he's been forced into the service of the Citadel.'

There was a brief silence, after which he said in a small, hesitant voice:

'While the fighting was going on ... what did I do?'

She frowned at him in the flickering light.

'I thought you'd heard enough about yourself,' she said

'Tell me anyway,' he said reluctantly.

She sighed and pulled her cloak more tightly around her.

'You did what we expected of you,' she said sadly. 'Instead of trying to defend your own flesh and blood, as any normal person would have done, you ran for the woods - thinking only of yourself, as usual. You would probably have got clean away if it hadn't been for that foot of yours. But before you could reach the top of the slope, one of the soldiers took off after you. By the look of that head, he caught up with you somewhere in the woods. Though in my opinion you were lucky to get off so lightly.'

When he didn't answer, she looked at him curiously.

'If I didn't know you better,' she said with forced lightness, 'I'd say you were feeling genuinely ashamed of yourself. But you always were a good actor.'

'I wish I was acting,' he said unhappily.

'Well, whatever the truth might be,' she said, 'it doesn't matter any longer. There's no changing the way things are. The best thing we can do now is get some rest. I suggest one of us tends the fire while the other sleeps.'

He nodded miserably, though at that moment he didn't feel particularly like sleeping.

'I'll take the first watch,' he said.

Again she looked at him curiously, but she didn't argue. Pointing up at the night sky, she said:

'Do you see that star? Wake me when it's directly overhead.'

Then, wrapping herself even more tightly in her tattered cloak, she lay down close to the fire and fell instantly asleep.

Watching her, Derin was struck by the strange calm which settled onto her features in sleep. Her face in repose was strikingly honest and open, making it impossible for him to doubt what she had told him. Yet it wasn't her face alone which persuaded him of the truth of her account. There was also his own response to her words. Somehow, he knew inside himself that what she had told him was true. That in itself was odd, because he could not actually recall the events she had described. While she had been speaking, the only clear image which had come into his mind had been the face of his father. All the rest - the soldiers, the ensuing fight, his own shameful cowardice - had been little more than words. But for all that, they had been words which had struck a familiar chord in his mind. It was almost as if he had heard them once before, long ago, spoken by somebody he trusted completely.

Shaking his head in bewilderment, he looked up at the dark sky. The star still had some distance to travel before it would be overhead. He threw another piece of wood into the flames and leaned back, resting his head against the cold stone of the wall. With eyes closed, he listened to the whisper of the wind and to the small furtive noises of the fire as it slowly burned down. Soon it would flicker out altogether, leaving him alone in total darkness and silence. To his surprise, he found himself waiting for that moment, unable to move. He thought, I have to help him . . . have to . . . For now he wasn't listening to the wind or to the slight rustlings of the camp fire, but rather to the crackle of flames above his head and to the clamour of fighting outside. With a cry of protest, he sprang up and ran over to the door. But there were no strange soldiers outside as he had expected, no struggling figures: the scene was deserted except for his father who was walking calmly away across the untrampled snow. He looked back only once, as though appealing to his son, his eyes begging him to follow. Then he disappeared into the winter landscape.

'No! Don't leave, come back!' he tried to shout.

But although he mouthed the words, no sound came out. And with a start he awoke to find that the day had broken and that Marna was standing over him.

'I see your loss of memory hasn't made you less selfish,' she said bitterly. 'If I hadn't woken in the night, the fire would have gone out altogether.'

He rose sheepishly to his feet, feeling cold and stiff. The fire was still burning, but there was very little fuel left.

'I'll collect some more wood,' he said hastily, limping towards the doorway.

But she called him back.

'There's no point,' she said. 'We have nothing to cook - nothing to remain here for.' She looked at him inquiringly. 'I've already decided where I shall go. What do you intend doing with yourself?'

He hesitated only briefly, for the second or two it took him to recall his dream. It came back to him in vivid detail: the smooth untrampled snow; the familiar figure standing there, appealing to him before he disappeared into the surrounding whiteness; his own unheeded cry of concern. And in that instant he knew beyond any shadow of doubt what had to be done.

'I shall go in search of my father,' he said quietly.

'A lot of good that will do,' she said sarcastically. 'You showed what you're worth yesterday, when you ran off and left him.'

'That's all in the past,' he said defensively. 'I can't excuse it or explain it away. All I can do is try to make up for it in the future.'

Marna scratched her head, clearly puzzled by his reply.

'Do you expect me to believe . . . ?' she began, and stopped - for Derin was already limping determinedly towards the doorway.

‘Where do you think you’re going?’ she asked sharply.

‘I’ve told you,’ he said. ‘To find my father.’

‘But you don’t even know where he is.’

‘Last night you mentioned the plains,’ he said. ‘I’ll look for him there.’

‘The plains!’ she broke out. ‘When you can’t even walk a mile without a crutch!’

‘I’ll manage,’ he called back angrily.

But he soon saw the folly of his own reply, for within a few paces he was floundering in the deep snow. Almost to his relief she called for him to stop.

‘Wait,’ she said, and hurried off up the slope, returning moments later with what was obviously a crutch, though he was not conscious of ever having seen it before.

‘Here,’ she said, ‘take it. You dropped it yesterday when you were trying to escape.’

It was a stout-looking stick worn smooth with use, V-shaped and padded at one end, and with a heavy metal tip at the other. He slipped it suspiciously under his right arm, and to his surprise found that it was exactly the right length, the padded V-shape snuggling comfortably into his armpit.

‘Oh, it’s yours all right,’ she said, in response to his initial suspicion.

He mumbled his thanks, grudgingly, and again turned away.

‘So you’re still determined to search for him?’ she asked.

‘Yes,’ he said shortly.

She sighed, grumbling softly to herself.

‘Oh well, I suppose I’d better come with you,’ she said at last.

‘There’s no need,’ he said, his former resentment flaring out again.

‘Don’t worry,’ she replied, ‘I’m not doing you a favour. I also intend searching for him. I decided that yesterday. So for the time being we might as well keep each other company – at least until I find out what game you’re playing.’

He didn’t reply, and together they walked away from the ruined farmhouse – Derin more slowly because he was searching the area of trampled snow (the scene of the previous day’s struggle) for some kind of weapon with which to protect himself during the journey ahead. There wasn't much to choose from: mainly splintered spear-shafts and shattered swords. The best he could find was an old long-bladed dagger, rusty and blunt, its edges badly hacked. It wasn't exactly what he was looking for, but it was the only weapon still intact. While he was weighing it uncertainly in his hand, trying to decide whether it was worth keeping, Marna said sneeringly:

'What use will that be against the soldiers of the plain? It's old and worn out. For years we've used it in the kitchen for splitting the light kindling. That's all it's good for.'

Possibly it was her sneering tone which decided him. He noticed a battered leather scabbard lying near by; and with sudden resolution he tied this to his belt and slipped the dagger into it.

'If you really need a weapon,' she added, 'what's wrong with the stick under your arm? Look at the weight of that metal tip. It would be far more effective than a worn-out dagger.'

Even then he might have given way, but it occurred to him that perhaps she had a special reason for wishing him to remain unarmed. And pointedly ignoring her arguments, he walked on.

With the crutch to help him he found walking much easier, and he didn't stop again until they reached the road at the bottom of the slope. Then he turned briefly in order to look back at the remains of the house which had sheltered him for so many years. Yet oddly enough it wasn't the ruined farmhouse which caught his eye: instead, it was the mark which the heavy metal tip of the crutch had made in the snow. The pattern was quite unmistakable: it was of a ten-pointed star enclosed by a circle. Instantly his mind flew back to the moment of his awakening in the wood on the previous afternoon. He had noticed an equally distinctive mark in the snow then, made by whoever had followed him. That person, whoever he or she was, must have carried a stick not unlike his own. He struggled to recall the exact pattern made by the metal tip - struggled ... and failed. He knew only that if he ever saw it again he would surely recognize it.

'Come on,' Marna grumbled. 'We have a long way to go and I'm getting cold standing here.'

Stifling the questions which rose to his lips, he tightened his grip on the crutch and followed her slowly down the road. To all appearances he was not so very different from the boy who had stumbled out of the wood. But now there was a more thoughtful look in his eyes. Something, some deep sense of suspicion, warned him that his present situation was not quite as simple as it appeared to be.

2. The Witch People

There had been no further snowfalls during the night and they had little difficulty in following the jumble of footprints left by the departing soldiers. The trail led straight down the road in the direction of the distant village, and for the first few minutes Derin looked keenly about him, searching for any sign of that half-remembered pattern which he had noticed in the woods. But now the snow was too badly scuffed by the heavy boots of the soldiers, and soon he gave up the search as hopeless.

It was hard, slow work walking through the deep snow and they had covered only a short distance by the time the sun rose above the horizon. As its light flooded across the landscape, glinting and sparkling on the clear white surface, Marna stopped in the middle of the road and sniffed the sharp morning air. When she breathed out, the white mist of her breath billowed around her head like a frosty halo.

'The winter's drawing to a close,' she said. 'The spring will be upon us soon. One more day, perhaps two, and the thaw will set in.'

Derin, who was watching her carefully, felt again that deep sense of suspicion which he had experienced earlier.

'They say that only witches can read the weather,' he said quietly. 'It's one of their gifts.'

He was vaguely aware that what he had said was an accusation, though he wasn't sure why, and he expected Marna to turn on him angrily. But she merely laughed, a high shrill cackle of sound which seemed to stir the snow on the hedgerows.

'What nonsense you talk, boy,' she said, still chuckling to herself. 'If I'm a witch, where's my staff? You're the only person carrying a stick: perhaps it's you who belongs to the Witch People.'

Again she went off into peals of laughter. He waited for her to stop and said:

'If you aren't a witch, how is it that you can tell the coming of the seasons?'

'How?' she answered, with just a trace of sharpness creeping into her voice. 'I'll tell you how. I trust my senses. Look around you. What has happened to that icy wind? Why is the sky cloudless for the first time in weeks? Can't you feel the growing warmth of the sun upon your cheek? Those are the signs I trust. There's nothing magical about them, not in the sense you mean.'

'Maybe so,' he said.

But Marna wasn't ready to leave the matter there.

'Once, not so very long ago,' she said, 'to call someone a witch was to pay them a compliment. Witch People and wise people meant the same thing. But these are troubled times, everything topsy-turvy, and the word witch could now cost somebody their life. So you be careful about making accusations.'

To emphasize her words, she wagged one finger sternly at him, in warning, before shuffling off through the snow. Half convinced, Derin followed. But only a few minutes later something happened which again made him begin to wonder about her.

They had reached a point where the narrow road ran between high banks when suddenly they were startled by a low cry. Instantly Marna whirled around, allowing her cloak to fall open as she made rapid, precise movements in the air with her hands.

'Quick, Derin, defend yourself!' she whispered fiercely.

Confused, not sure of which way to turn, he drew the battered old dagger and stood at the ready.

There was a short silence and then the low murmuring cry was heard again - though now it was clearly a cry of pain. Without hesitation, Marna scrambled up the high bank and pushed through the leafless hedge. Derin, following her, saw a man lying in the shelter of a fallen tree. He was obviously a soldier for he was dressed in a rusty coat of chain-mail which he wore over a thick woollen tunic. He had no helmet or weapons, but someone, perhaps one of his comrades, had placed a leather jerkin beneath him to protect him from the cold. He didn't move as they approached. His face was deathly pale, his lips pinched and blue. From the upper part of his chest, just below the collar-bone, the thin shaft of an arrow protruded.

Marna stood quite still for a moment, looking down at him. Her face wore a mixed expression of anger and sadness.

'So this is how the soldiers of the plain are now rewarded for their services,' she said indignantly. 'They are left here to die without help or companionship.' She turned towards Derin. 'You see why I also wish to find your father. It is this that we have to save him from.'

'Is he really dying?' Derin asked in a whisper - though he knew the answer to his question without needing to be told. The only wonder was how the man had survived for so long.

The soldier moaned again and Marna stooped down and filled her toothless mouth with snow. When it was melted, she made a cup of her hand and squirted the water into it. Then, gently raising the man's head, she allowed the warm water to dribble between his lips. He coughed and swallowed twice, the effort causing spasms of pain to pass across his face. For a moment or two he seemed to revive. Mumbling what sounded like words of gratitude, he looked up at Marna who hovered above him. But at the sight of her face, a wild, terrified look came into his eyes.

'Spare me!' he cried out. 'No more! Mercy, mercy, mercy ...'

It was the last word he spoke. His head fell sideways, and with a barely perceptible tremor his body slumped into an attitude of death.

As Marna leaned forward to close his eyes, Derin, the dagger still in his hand, inched nervously back towards the hedge.

'He was frightened of you!' he said in a horrified voice. 'Why of you?'

Marna didn't answer. She was gazing steadily towards the east and all at once she appeared to have grown older and very tired.

'So close,' she murmured to herself, 'already so close.'

'Answer me!' Derin almost shouted. 'Why was he terrified of you?'

Marna turned around and noticed with surprise that the trembling point of the dagger was directed at her. She clicked her tongue in disapproval.

'You have nothing to fear from me,' she said softly, 'nobody has ... except perhaps for one person ... only one.'

'Who is that?' he asked.

Again she didn't answer - though Derin sensed that she wasn't consciously ignoring him: her mind seemed to be elsewhere, wrestling with some problem he didn't understand.

'Come, we must be on our way,' she said at last, rising stiffly to her feet. 'There's nothing more we can do here, and we must keep moving if we hope to reach the village of Sone before nightfall.'

Gently, and without any sign of fear, she reached out and turned the point of the dagger aside.

'Whatever differences we may have had,' she said, 'there's never been any violence between us. Nor will there ever be. My word on that.'

And to Derin's amazement she put one arm affectionately around his shoulders, hugging him briefly, before passing back through the hedge and clambering down onto the road.

Yet despite that unusual show of affection, in the hours which followed she remained distant from him, unwilling to talk, a troubled, withdrawn expression on her face. The only thing which seemed to arouse her was any unexpected sound or movement - a flock of birds flying swiftly overhead or the crack of a dry branch breaking under its weight of snow. Then she would stop in midstride and glance warily about her, her old hands raised as though ready to fend off some unseen evil.

Nor was she alone in sensing the presence of danger. During the course of the morning they passed a number of farmhouses. Several of them were deserted, but the few people they did see refused even to raise a hand in greeting. At the first sight of strangers on the road they ran inside and closed the doors. It was as though fear and distrust, like the fields of snow and the stark leafless trees, had become a visible part of the winter landscape.

Around midday they again came to a farmhouse, this one set slightly back from the road. It was obviously inhabited because a curl of smoke rose from the chimney. Derin, who was tired and hungry, imagined the warm interior, the cooking pots hanging over the fire.

'Can't we stop and beg for food?' he asked.

'Don't be a fool, boy,' Marna replied scornfully. 'These are country people, shy of strangers at the best of times, and it's only a day since the soldiers passed by, bullying and frightening them and carrying off their menfolk. What answer do you think we'd receive?'

'But we have to get food from somewhere,' Derin objected.

By way of answer, Marna produced a small cloth bag from under her cloak. Inside it were the remains of the porridge they had cooked the night before. Lumpy and cold, it appeared more unappetizing than ever.

'This will have to satisfy you until we reach Sone,' she said, handing it to him.

Derin looked hesitantly at the grey, tasteless morsel and glanced again at the farmhouse. The curl of smoke from the chimney, with its suggestion of warmth and comfort, seemed to signal invitingly to him.

'Foolish or not,' he said, 'there's no harm in asking for help.'

And putting the remains of the porridge into his pocket, he limped through the deeply trodden snow to the front door.

Close up, the house was less inviting. The small panes in the front window had been smashed and pieces of dirty sacking had been crammed into the gaps. There was also a musty smell about the place which conveyed to Derin an atmosphere of poverty and misery. He was almost tempted to give up there and then, to go straight back to where Marna was waiting impatiently for him. But after a moment's hesitation he decided that having come this far he had nothing to lose by asking. And reaching out, he knocked lightly on the door.

At first there was no reply. Only when he had knocked several times did he hear any movement inside. Then a voice called out:

'Go away. Leave us.'

Whoever it was sounded frightened and upset, on the verge of tears.

'We won't do you any harm,' he called out.

He waited, and when he received no response he added:

'We're cold and hungry. Could you spare us anything to eat?'

Still nobody answered, and he raised his crutch and beat more loudly on the door with the metal tip. But at the first blow the door creaked open of its own accord, as though it had not been properly latched. With his hand on the hilt of his dagger, Derin stepped cautiously into the gloomy interior. In the poor light, which came mainly from the fire at the far end of the room, he saw a jumble of smashed furniture and pieces of broken crockery littering the earth floor. Standing against the opposite wall, in the deepest shadow, was a young woman. She was hollow-eyed, thin and pale, and was clutching what appeared to be a bundle of rags. Only when she shuffled forward did he realize that she was holding a tiny infant which was suckling at her breast.

'They've taken everything already,' she said. 'I have nothing more to give.'

'They?' he asked.

'The soldiers,' she answered, starting to cry. 'We tried to keep them out, but they forced the door. They did this' – she indicated the broken furniture – 'to teach us a lesson. That's what they said. Then they took my husband and all the food and left.'

'You have nobody here to help you?' Derin asked.

She shook her head, wiping the tears from her cheeks with the back of her hand. Again she shuffled forward a few steps, looking past Derin to where Marna waited on the road. Up until that moment she had appeared ready to trust him, perhaps sensing that he meant her no harm. But at the sight of Marna her eyes widened in terror and she backed away, trying to hide herself in the shadows.

'No!' she said, as though imploring him, 'no!'

Derin also glanced behind him, to where Marna was pacing to and fro, stamping her feet to keep them warm. In her long tattered cloak and with her great bush of unruly grey hair, she looked a wild enough figure; but not someone to inspire this kind of terror.

'What is it?' he asked.

'They warned us,' the woman said in an hysterical voice, 'the soldiers told us what the Witch People could do. But when you came in I didn't know that you ... that you ...'

Unable to go on, she clutched at the tiny child in her arms, drawing it protectively against her thin bosom.

'We're just poor people like you,' he protested, 'we won't do anything to hurt you.'

But he could see that she wasn't listening to him. Made deaf by her own terror, she cowered back against the wall like a cornered animal.

'If I can do anything to help ...' he began, and stopped again. Words at such a moment seemed so inadequate. And on impulse he reached into his pocket and took out the cold fragment of porridge which he had spurned only a few minutes earlier.

'Here,' he said gently, pulling aside the cloth and holding it out towards her.

She seemed not to understand him to begin with.

'Here,' he said again, 'it's food, take it.'

She looked then at his hand and slowly, as she realized what he was offering her, the terror left her face and was replaced by a look of wonder.

'For me?' she whispered, unbelieving.

'It's little enough,' he said apologetically, 'but it's all we have.'

She reached forward, hungrily, and again drew back as though suspecting some trap.

'You have nothing to fear,' he said, 'we wouldn't trick you.'

Still with the baby clutched tightly against her, she crept towards him.

'Then it's not true, what the soldiers said,' she murmured, as much to herself as to him. 'They told us, beware of the Witch People, they'll kill the person inside you, they'll make you dead inside. Like that other one who came here, looking. Dead inside. But it's not true; it's still the way it used to be. Our friends still ... our friends.'

And before he could stop her, she fell to her knees and kissed his outstretched hand, pulling it passionately towards her, so that he felt the warmth of the child through the rags which covered it. Hastily, he snatched his hand away, accidentally dropping the small parcel of food on the floor. With a single eager movement, she swept it up as though it too were a living child. She was crying again, but now she was shedding tears of gratitude.

'The blessed ones,' she said brokenly, 'the blessed ...'

'No!' he interrupted loudly, almost shouting at her. 'I'm not worthy of this!'

For suddenly all he could think of were the things Marna had said of him - how she had described him as selfish and lazy, considering nobody but himself.

'You don't understand!' he broke out. 'I don't deserve this! I'm a coward; I deserted him!'

But his words had no effect on the figure kneeling at his feet. She stretched forward, trying to kiss his hand once more, and he quickly turned and hurried from the house, pulling the door firmly closed behind him, as though by so doing he could shut away his own deep sense of shame.

Marna was still pacing impatiently to and fro when he reached the road.

'Well?' she asked him as he limped towards her.

In spite of the coldness of the day, he found that his forehead was damp with sweat.

'There was only a poor woman and a child inside,' he said, trying to sound unperturbed. 'They had nothing to give us – they had nothing even for themselves.'

'It was as I thought,' Marna said. 'Never mind, let's eat what little we have and then be on our way.'

There was an awkward silence.

'What's the matter with you, boy?' she asked sternly.

'I no longer have the food,' he admitted.

'You don't have it?' Marna said, not understanding. 'What have you done with it?'

'I . . . I gave it to the woman,' he murmured, gazing down at his feet.

He was waiting for a rebuke. But Marna merely strode over towards him. Putting her hand roughly under his chin, she jerked his head upwards so that she could look full into his face.

'I see you do have a conscience after all,' she said. 'The guilt of the past weighs heavily upon you. Is this how you hope to wipe out that guilt? With small acts of mercy?'

'It wasn't only guilt,' he protested, though he knew that what she said was at least partly true.

'What else prompted you?' she asked doubtfully.

He remembered the woman's terror-stricken face, hollow and pale with misery and hunger.

'It was also . . .' he began.

But before he could finish there was a whirr of wings overhead. They both looked up and saw a large black raven flying towards them. It circled twice, spiralling down, and landed only a few feet from where they stood. It showed no fear of them, its head cocked on one side, its beady eye staring at them intently.

'What does it want?' Derin asked in wonder.

'Be still,' Marna cautioned him.

And taking a step forward, she crouched down and put her hand out towards the bird. But it merely pecked at her fingers - not viciously: just hard enough to warn her to keep her distance.

She turned to Derin.

'You're the one that it's watching,' she said. 'Come closer, here beside me.'

Derin also stepped forward and crouched down.

'Now put out your hand,' she directed him.

He hesitated, wary of the long black beak which ended in a sharp point.

'Have you so little courage,' she asked sarcastically, 'you who hope to rescue your father from the soldiers?'

Stung by the implied insult, he placed his hand on the snow beside the bird. This time it showed no aggression. Stepping onto the proffered hand, it walked deliberately up his arm and settled itself comfortably on his shoulder. Startled, Derin watched the creature out of the corner of his eye. Its cruel beak was only inches from his unprotected face, but strangely he felt in no danger. He didn't even flinch when the bird suddenly opened its beak and let out a loud cry:

'Craak.'

Despite his astonishment he couldn't help laughing.

'Craak,' he mimicked, smiling at Marna. 'That would be a good name for him. Don't you think so, Marna?'

She fingered her chin thoughtfully, considering the boy and the bird together.

'I see your talent hasn't left you,' she said.

'What talent?' he asked, puzzled.

'The gift of charming the wild creatures of the countryside,' she explained. 'You've always had it, ever since you were a small child. Always filling the house with wild foxes and mice and rabbits and whatever else you could find in the woods.'

He looked again at the way the bird sat placidly upon his shoulder, its feathers ruffled up against the cold.

'But surely this creature isn't wild,' he said.

'Perhaps not,' Marna conceded.

'Then why should it come to us like this?'

Marna turned around and faced the south, the direction from which the bird had flown. Her eyes were fixed upon the distant horizon and a worried frown creased her forehead.

'It could be a portent of good or of evil,' she said warningly.

'You mean the bird might be evil?' he asked, momentarily alarmed.

'Ah no,' she breathed out, 'the bird itself is a good sign. What worries me is the reason for its coming to us.'

'I don't understand you,' he said. 'Are you saying that something evil may have happened to make the bird fly here? Is that it?'

She shrugged.

'Who knows,' she said.

And without any warning she suddenly started to laugh, the same high thin cackle she had made earlier in the day - except that now it sounded hollow and unconvincing, like the laughter of someone trying to hide some secret disquiet.

'But you must have some idea of what brought it here?' he insisted.

'Why not try asking the bird?' she replied, continuing to laugh.

The bird, silent until then, wiped its beak on Derin's hair and moved its feet restlessly.

'Craak,' was all it said.

3. A Shadow

They reached the village of Sone, footsore and weary, just as the sun was setting. In the faded yellow light of late afternoon they entered the main street and made their way to the inn which stood at the far end. It was a low building with broad eaves, and despite the snow which was banked up against its walls it looked snug and secure. Pushing open the heavy oak door, they peered inside: the lamps had not yet been lit, but there was a roaring fire in the big open hearth. Only one customer was there ahead of them – a man sitting in the corner furthest away from the fire. He wore a thick woollen muffler over much of his face, as though he too had only just come in from the cold, and he didn't turn or look up as they entered. The only other person inside was the landlord: a short fat man with bright dark eyes and black hair, which suggested he must originally have been one of the woodland people.

Unlike the woman in the farmhouse he didn't appear alarmed by Marna's sudden entrance, though he obviously knew her. He merely nodded a curt greeting, a frown of disapproval on his dark chubby face, and glanced briefly at Derin who still carried Craak on his shoulder.

'Why have you come here?' he said softly, taking care that his voice should not reach as far as the man sitting in the corner. 'You know it's dangerous. The roads and villages are guarded and the soldiers are everywhere, searching for the Witch People.'

'And why should that worry us?' Marna asked, a mischievous smile on her wrinkled face.

'This is no time for joking,' he said seriously, wiping his small fat hands on his apron. 'The only safe place for you is back at the farmhouse.'

'There is no longer any farmhouse,' Marna said. 'The soldiers burned it down yesterday.'

'Even a burned-out farmhouse is safer than the highways and villages,' the landlord answered quickly. 'There is deep trouble in the land. It is being said that the Council of Iri-Nan and the sacred Circle of the Grove are at war – the people of the plains and those of the mountains pitted against each other, as in the old times.'

'And do you believe that to be true?' Marna asked, her own face growing suddenly serious.

The landlord shrugged his plump shoulders.

'Some of it may be talk, but certainly there are strangers abroad and men are dying on the roads hereabouts. That is partly why the soldiers are here: not only to recruit more men, but also to keep the uplands under the firm control of the Council. When the elders in the villages complain, the soldiers claim they are only here to protect us. Meanwhile they suspect everybody of plotting against them, of secretly supporting the sacred Circle – the Witch People especially.'

'But surely they realize that is unlikely,' Marna replied. 'Witch People or not, we are all uplanders here. We are a separate community, proud of our independence. Why should we throw that independence away by needlessly siding with the powers in the mountains or on the plains? Unless of course ...'

She broke off abruptly. Yet the little man seemed to understand what she had been about to say.

'I also used to think as you do,' he said, 'but the fact is, during the past weeks I've stood in this very room night after night and heard upland farmers arguing hotly in favour of the Council or the Circle, almost as if they owed them some kind of allegiance. Whether you like it or not, there are plenty ready to take sides in these parts.'

'And are people still talking in this way?' Marna asked, a note of disbelief in her voice.

'That I couldn't tell you,' the landlord admitted. 'Very few farmers come here now. Most of the younger people have gone, and not all of them with the soldiers. A good many of the young men and women, so I hear, have run off to the mountains in order to aid the Circle, and of their own free will, what's more.' He spoke these last words in a whisper, his small dark eyes darting suspiciously from the door to the window and back again. 'That's why I call these troubled times,' he went on. 'If you ask me, the best thing is to stay out of it. Go back to your farm where you'll be safe. And take the boy with you.'

Up until then, Derin had remained in the background, listening to the whispered conversation without really understanding most of what was being said. Now he stepped forward.

'We can't return yet,' he said firmly. 'You see, the soldiers have taken my father with them.'

'Your father?' the landlord queried.

'The farmer called Ardelan,' Marna added quickly in explanation.

'Ah yes,' the landlord said, 'I saw him arrive here last night and he left again early this morning. There was a whole crowd of farming people, Ardelan amongst them, marching between two columns of soldiers. By now they'll be well on their way to the plains.'

'Did you have a chance to speak to him?' Derin asked.

But at that moment there was a sound of someone kicking the snow off heavy boots just outside the door. Before they could hide or even move, the door opened and a soldier came in. Like most of the plainsmen, he was tall and sparely built, with long pale features and lank blond hair that poked out at the bottom of his helmet. At the sight of Marna and Derin he paused for a second or two, inspecting them carefully, before coming over to where they stood close to the fire.

'And what have we here?' he said suspiciously.

There was a hint of a smile on his thin lips, but his light blue eyes remained cold and distant.

'They're just farming people,' the landlord said hastily, an unmistakable tremor of fear in his voice.

'Just farming people?' the soldier asked doubtfully. 'Nothing more?'

'They've come here begging for food,' the landlord explained.

And he bustled behind the counter and produced two large loaves of bread which he thrust into Marna's arms.

'The blessing of many good seasons upon you,' Marna said, and bowing low in gratitude she turned as if to go.

But the soldier, hands on hips, had already stepped between her and the door.

'If you're farming people,' he said, 'what are you doing here begging? Haven't you food enough where you've come from?'

Marna gave him a fierce, unbending look.

'We had more than enough until the soldiers burned our farmhouse to the ground,' she said angrily. 'Now, thanks to the likes of you, we're reduced to this.'

Again she tried to make for the door and again he stepped into her way.

'Not so fast, old woman,' he said. 'Tell me first why the boy bears a bird on his shoulder.'

'He found it in the snow,' she explained. 'It was cold and hungry, like us. He cared for it and now it won't leave him. Isn't that so, boy?'

Derin nodded dumbly. His mouth felt sour and dry and he didn't trust himself to speak.

'And I suppose this is something you also found in the snow,' the soldier said.

Before Marna could stop him, he pulled her cloak open at the front, revealing her long black dress.

'Well?' he asked threateningly.

'I'm an old woman,' Marna replied humbly, 'too old to work for a living. I have to accept whatever clothes people offer me.'

'Do you take me for an idiot?' the soldier suddenly shouted, his pale face turning almost white with anger. 'Don't you think I recognize you for what you are, the pair of you? You're Witch People!' And he spat on the ground with disgust. 'It's because of you and your kind that so many soldiers are lying out there dead in the snow at this moment!'

'There you're mistaken,' Marna corrected him proudly. 'In these parts the Witch People are healers, curing the sick and diseased. Their task is not to kill, but rather to save others from death.'

'Do you expect me to believe that?' the soldier said scornfully. 'Haven't I seen my comrades fall in the snow, while one of your kind slinks away? Well, you won't escape this time. We'll make a public example of you. We'll show the inhabitants of this village what happens to those who support the power of the Grove.'

While the soldier was talking, Derin's hand slid slowly towards the hilt of his dagger. He knew that he must act soon, but he dreaded the moment of decision. Above all, he feared that his nerve might fail as it had on the previous day when he had run away into the woods. As if sensing what was in his mind, Marna turned towards him and placed a restraining hand on his arm.

'Come, boy,' she said, 'we're caught and there's nothing we can do about it.'

And bending over, she placed the two loaves on the floor at her feet, leaving both hands free.

'No tricks now,' the soldier said warningly.

But he was too late. She had already straightened up, and as she did so she made a rapid passing movement with her hands. The effect was instantaneous. All the anger and hatred vanished from the soldier's face and he was left looking dazed and bewildered, more like a lost child than a grown man. Watching him, Derin wondered briefly whether he too might have looked something like that when he had woken in the woods. But in the heat of the moment the thought was gone before he could grasp and consider it. Marna was already saying in an innocent voice:

'We're just poor farming people, you understand, nothing more.'

The soldier, obviously confused, put one hand to his forehead and blinked rapidly.

'Yes,' he said uncertainly, 'poor farming people ... my apologies ... I understand now.'

And still shaking his head in bewilderment, he turned and left the inn.

'That was a foolish thing to do.' It was the landlord speaking from behind them. 'When he realizes what has been done to him, he will only distrust and hate you the more.'

'That may be so,' Marna agreed, 'but by then we should be far from here.'

'Do you really think you can escape the soldiers?' he asked.

'We shall try,' she replied.

She had already retrieved the loaves and walked over to the door.

'One question before you go,' the landlord called after her. 'The bird which the boy carries - why did it come to him?'

Marna looked back, her hand poised over the latch of the door.

'You come from the woodlands originally?' she asked.

The landlord nodded.

'Then you know as much as I,' she said. 'I too can only guess. It may be that the soldiers discovered the bird's original owner.'

'And if that is not the case?'

'There are other possibilities,' she said darkly, 'some of them preferable, others far more frightening.'

And before the landlord could answer she had stepped out into the night.

Derin, who was still lingering by the fire, hurried after her. But just as he reached the door, there was a slight sound behind him and he looked back. The man who had been sitting in the far corner was standing only feet away from him, his face still muffled in a woollen scarf, only the eyes clearly visible. Involuntarily, Derin gasped and stood quite still. In all his life he had never seen such eyes: they were blank and strangely unseeing, like deep pools of black water - or like the eyes of the dead. For a few seconds, as he gazed into them, time seemed almost to stop. Vaguely he was aware that at the very bottom of those deep pools something stirred, something secret and hidden, which was spying on him. But when he probed deeper, searching for that hidden presence, he saw only himself, lying on the snow in the woods. Unable to tear his eyes away, he watched, fascinated, as this exact likeness of himself awoke and looked wonderingly about him, his own familiar features clearly revealing a sense of inner confusion and emptiness. On impulse he wanted to reach out and comfort this other self which continued to gaze without recognition or understanding at the gaunt trees and grey, lowering sky. But before he could move, there was a flurry of wings from somewhere near by and a sharp protesting cry from Craak. And just as abruptly as it had appeared, so now the scene dissolved and vanished. Once again he found himself back inside the inn, staring into the dead eyes of this man he had never seen before. Nothing, it seemed, had changed - except perhaps for Craak, who was moving restlessly on his shoulder. And yet he now felt weak and drained, as though something had been drawn out of him against his will, his memory somehow probed and searched.

'What ... what do you want of me?' he said falteringly.

But instead of answering, the man stepped quickly past him and disappeared into the darkness.

It took Derin several moments to recover, and then he too staggered outside.

'What's been keeping you, boy?' Marna asked irritably.

She was standing in the deep shadow of the eaves, waiting for him.

'That man,' he said, 'where did he go?'

He looked up and down the narrow street, but it was empty.

'What are you bothering yourself about a stranger for?' she asked, still with a trace of irritation in her voice.

'You should have seen him,' Derin said. 'His eyes – they were ... they were dead.'

Marna was instantly alert, peering into the surrounding darkness.

'Dead, you say?' she asked him urgently.

Suddenly he remembered something that had been said earlier that day, by the poor half-starved woman in the cottage.

'Yes,' he answered, 'it was just as if he was dead inside.'

'And you looked at him?' Marna asked. 'Stared into his eyes?'

'Only for a moment,' he said.

'Even a moment can be too long,' she said quickly. 'Tell me, what did you see?'

'Myself, lying on the snow in the woods, after I'd run away.'

'Did you see anything before that time? The days before the soldiers came, perhaps?'

'No, nothing more.'

She didn't reply, and it was difficult for him to see what effect his words had on her because her face was hidden in shadow. He heard her muttering to herself:

'Bad ... bad ... a bad sign.'

'How do you mean, a bad sign?' he asked her.

But she turned on him angrily.

'There's no time to talk now,' she said. 'We must get away from here as quickly as possible.'

And with the two loaves tucked under one arm and with her free hand clutching Derin's left wrist, she led him hurriedly down a lane which ran alongside the inn.

The village itself was only five streets wide and they were soon out in the open countryside, floundering through the deep snow. A thin moon had risen, and guided by its feeble light they made for a dense cluster of trees about a mile west of the village and well away from the road. There, hidden from prying eyes, they stopped for the night, Marna unexpectedly producing a small tinderbox from under her cloak and rapidly lighting a fire. Crouched over the warming flames they broke off pieces of bread from one of the loaves and ate them in silence. It was the only food they had had all day, and not until their hunger was satisfied did they sit back and look inquiringly at each other.

'Well?' Marna asked, a smile creasing her old face.

Derin's mind was so full of questions that he hardly knew where to begin.

'You told me this morning that you weren't one of the Witch People,' he said, 'and yet there, in the inn, you showed that you are.'

Marna reached up with both hands and smoothed down her wild bush of grey hair.

'Was it so very bad of me to deny it?' she said. 'After all, I carry no staff and I've lived an ordinary enough life for the past twelve years - caring for you, cleaning your father's house, cooking for you both.'

'But still you lied to me,' Derin said doggedly.

'You can call it a lie if you wish,' she conceded, 'though bear in mind that earlier today I didn't know whether I could trust you.'

'And now you do?' he asked.

'I no longer have any choice,' she replied. 'From the moment the soldier entered the inn and accused us, we've both been wanted people. There's no going back now, for either of us. If we are to survive, we have to trust and rely on each other, whether we like the idea or not.'

She spoke with such grim certainty that Derin stood up and paced uneasily round to the other side of the fire.

'Oh, I know what you're thinking,' she added. 'You're wondering how you can possibly travel with a witch. Well, my answer to that is simple - why not? The soldiers already suspect us both, so you have little to lose. And what I said at the inn is true: here in the uplands the Witch People are not a force for evil, whatever others may think. We have nothing to do with the cruelty and death which you witnessed on the road today.'

Still Derin remained on the other side of the fire, undecided, pulling uncertainly at his lower lip. Seen through the flames, Marna did indeed look like a witch, with her withered, sunken lips, her long unkempt grey hair, and her eyes glinting at him in the firelight.

'Before you decide what course to take,' she went on, 'there is one other thing you should consider – and that is what we are doing here. Our main aim is to rescue your father, don't forget that. And as things stand, two people together have a far greater chance of success than either of us working alone.'

'But why should you wish to rescue him?' Derin asked suspiciously.

'He has shown me twelve years of kindness,' she replied. 'That is reason enough.'

Not without hesitation, Derin nodded his agreement.

'Very well,' he said, 'we'll remain together – but only on one condition. You spoke just now of trust. If you really meant that, then prove it to me: tell me what's going on, because I understand almost nothing. Why did the bird fly to me today? Who is the man with dead eyes and why does he look like that? Why do the soldiers hate the Witch People? What were you and ...?'

He faltered and stopped as Marna held up her hand for silence.

'I can give you a reliable answer to only one of your questions,' she said. 'The soldiers hate us because for some reason they associate us with the power which lies to the east, high in the mountains – the power of the sacred Circle, which dwells beside the Grove. As for the answers to your other questions, I can only offer guesses; and in my experience it is often both dangerous and unwise to guess about things we don't fully understand. Therefore, what I propose is this: that for the present I tell you only what I know with certainty.'

'I agree to that,' Derin answered, and he came back and sat beside her on the fallen log they had dragged close to the fire.

Marna made herself as comfortable as she could, lifted her long skirt up to her knees so that she could warm her legs at the flames.

'A great many years ago,' she began, 'when my own grandmother was still a child, this whole area was torn by war. There was bloodshed and cruelty everywhere – from the mountains to the sea, from the southern plains to the uplands.'

'What caused the war?' Derin asked.

'I'm coming to that,' she explained patiently. 'In those days there were only two rulers ... well, I suppose you could call them both rulers, of sorts. On the plains, in the city of Iri-Nan, which is where we're heading now, there was a King; and in the eastern mountains there was someone called the Warden of the Grove. Each of these two rulers or leaders had a different kind of authority. The King made laws, imposed taxes, and governed the everyday lives of his subjects. The Warden of the Grove, on the other hand, possessed no land or riches, and nor did he tell the people what to do. Yet he was still a great power in the land. With a single wave of his Staff he could cure widespread sickness or persuade the rain to fall on parched soil or make the crops fruitful in times of famine. It is claimed by some that the Witch People still retain a little of his power.'

'And was it these two rulers who went to war?' Derin broke in.

'Yes,' she answered sadly.

'But why?' he said, puzzled. 'Their powers were so very different - what did they have to gain?'

'I suppose they disliked or were jealous of each other. Who can say for sure after all this time? Whatever the reason, the war between them was a long and bloody affair which left the land and the people exhausted. At the end of it all there was widespread misery and suffering: the King was dead, and so was the Warden of the Grove, together with thousands of their followers. The only good thing which came out of the war was that there now arose a single leader who combined the offices of King and Warden. His name was Wenborn the Wise, and he is still remembered with affection by the old people. His wisdom consisted mainly in this: that before he died, he devised a plan for preventing all future wars. In place of a King, he set up a Council; and instead of a single Warden, he appointed a holy Circle of elders.'

'But how was that supposed to prevent war?' Derin asked.

'Ah, that is where Wenborn was clever. He ruled that neither the Council nor the Circle could declare war unless every single member agreed. And even today, before anybody can become such a member, he or she has to take an oath to that effect. But Wenborn didn't stop there. In case that wasn't enough to guarantee peace, he built in one other safeguard. He decreed that the Council and the Circle should each contain ten members; yet only nine were ever to be present at one time. The tenth person, who was to remain unknown to the others, had to dwell amongst the people, his identity a secret to all but a chosen few. And of course, without that one essential member, the Circle or the Council could never be complete; it could only ever assemble as a group of nine; and as such it was not authorized to declare war. That unknown tenth person, therefore, whether of the Council or of the Circle, was intended as a kind of safety factor whose task was twofold: to remain hidden and to be ever watchful. Should the peace be threatened at any time, he or she would be responsible for the restoration of order and sanity.'

She stopped and leaned closer to the fire.

'And do this Council and Circle continue to rule today?' Derin asked.

'Yes. As far as I know, it is the Council in the city of Iri-Nan which has sent the soldiers here to the uplands.'

'But how can that be?' he objected. 'If what you say is true, and war is impossible, then their coming here doesn't make sense. For what else can you call it but war when soldiers overrun the land? Or when innocent people like my father are carried off against their will to serve in an army they don't support? Or when men die in the snow as that one did today?'

Marna sighed and patted him comfortingly on the knee.

'Perhaps you begin to see why I cannot give a confident answer to your questions,' she said. 'I too am puzzled . . . and troubled by what is happening around us.'

They sat staring into the fire, neither of them speaking for several minutes. Derin said at last:

'I've been thinking. Couldn't the Council or the Circle simply have broken their oath? That would explain the soldiers being here.'

'It's possible,' she answered shortly.

But there was an undertone of doubt in her voice which Derin could not ignore.

'You think it's unlikely, don't you?' he said.

She nodded.

'I find it hard to believe that nine people would all agree to break a sacred oath at once. If only one protested, surely some word of it would have leaked out.'

'Then what other explanation is there?' he asked, exasperated.

'There is one other distinct possibility,' she began, and stopped, clearly regretting having spoken.

'Go on,' Derin urged her.

She warmed her hands at the fire and then rubbed them deliberately together.

'I'm being foolish,' she said. 'It's best not to speak of such things.'

Derin rose abruptly to his feet.

'I thought we were supposed to be trusting each other,' he said.

'In this one matter,' she replied, 'you would do well to trust my silence.'

'But why?' he objected.

'Because words sometimes have a power of their own. Were I to voice what is in my mind, it is possible that the words I use might help to bring about the very evil I fear.' She paused. 'No, it is better that we wait. If what I dread is true, we shall find out soon enough.'

'These are just excuses!' he said indignantly. 'How can words alone possess any power?'

He thumped the end of his crutch down heavily in a gesture of annoyance - leaving a clear imprint in the snow of a star enclosed by a circle - and it was then, as if in answer to his last question, that the bird on his shoulder put its beak close to his ear and seemed almost to whisper the sound of 'craak'. It was, he knew instantly, a warning, and he whirled around and gazed into the darkness.

'Quick!' he said to Marna, 'a light!'

Moving with a speed which belied her age, she grabbed a burning stick from the fire and held it above her head.

'What is it?' she asked softly.

Derin stepped cautiously forward and scanned the spaces between the trees. A few yards from where he stood there was a deep pool of shadow, but it appeared so natural that he would probably have ignored it if the bird had not suddenly launched itself from his shoulder and swooped low over the darkened snow. Immediately, the innocent-looking shadow stirred, revealing itself as the body of a man. Startled, Derin placed a hand defensively on the hilt of his dagger; but the man merely scrambled to his feet and ran rapidly away through the trees. In the darkness, it was impossible to see him clearly, yet Derin did notice one thing: he was wearing a heavy woollen muffler around the lower part of his face.

Derin turned and limped slowly back into the circle of light.

'Who was it?' Marna asked anxiously.

'It was the man I saw at the inn; the one with the dead eyes.'

'Ah, so you already have a shadow,' she replied in a whisper. 'Then it is as well that I did not speak openly about my fears.'

4. Conflict

During the night a warm wind began to blow and by dawn the thaw had set in. As day broke they again set out across the uplands, wading now shin-deep through a slush of rapidly melting snow. Within an hour their leather boots were soaked through, but they continued to trudge on, moving slowly towards the south. In the wet, slippery conditions walking was hard work for both of them: Marna hampered by her age, Derin by his crutch which kept skidding out from under him. Again and again he slipped and fell into the cold slush, until soon his woollen clothes were almost as wet as his boots. At one point, nearly crying with vexation, he demanded that they stop and rest; but Marna, who seemed driven by a new sense of urgency, wouldn't hear of it.

'I thought yesterday that you'd left your whining, complaining ways behind you,' she said fiercely. 'But I see you're not so greatly changed after all.'

There was such scorn in her voice that Derin picked himself up without another word and moved off ahead of her.

Yet soon afterwards they had no choice but to stop for a while. They were following a parallel course to the road, which lay less than a mile to the east, when all at once they detected signs of movement in the distance. All around them the country was particularly open, offering little cover - even the nearest hedge was some way off - and Marna immediately signalled for Derin to get down. Lying side by side on the sodden ground, between patches of unmelted snow, they watched as a troop of soldiers moved rapidly along the road. While they waited, Marna broke off a little more of the bread she carried and handed him a piece.

'Here,' she said, 'this will help to keep you warm.'

It was the closest she had come to speaking kindly to him all morning and, despite the cold and wet and the unpleasantness of their present position, he felt oddly comforted. Gratefully, he ate the proffered bread; and some minutes later, the road clear at last, they rose and walked on.

After that initial scare they were far more watchful: ever on the lookout for soldiers; and careful to take advantage of whatever cover the uplands afforded. They even gave a wide berth to the isolated farmhouses they passed. That, perhaps, was an unnecessary precaution. There seemed to be no young men or women left to work the land, and the few old people they saw labouring in the fields ran off as they approached. Fear and distrust, here as elsewhere, were like a disease that had infected the very air people breathed.

By the end of the day they had reached a part of the uplands that was almost totally bare of trees, and the only refuge they could find was a tall hedge bordering a stream. Here they stopped for the night and struggled to light a small fire with pieces of damp wood torn from the hedge. As darkness fell, Marna lowered herself stiffly to the ground, groaning softly as she eased her old bones. Derin, too, was in some discomfort, the crutch having rubbed a raw patch under his arm; but after the reprimand he had received earlier he was determined not to complain. Only when he thought Marna wasn't looking did he dare to ease his wet clothing away from the sore spot. But he had reckoned without her sharp eyes.

'What's the matter with you, boy?' she asked.

She crawled over and inspected the injury for herself.

'Something had better be done about that,' she announced, 'or we'll have you unfit to travel in a day or two.'

'I'm sorry,' he said, shamefaced, 'I can't understand why it's happened in so short a time.'

'So short a time!' she took him up quickly, her voice growing suddenly shrill. 'What do you mean by that?'

'I mean after only two days,' he explained, startled by her manner. 'I thought I'd have been more used to the crutch after all these years.'

'Oh, is that all,' she said, sounding oddly relieved. 'Well, what do you expect? You were never an active child. If you'd been less idle all your life, this wouldn't have happened. Let it be a lesson to you.'

She continued to grumble on about how lazy and unreliable he'd been in the past. Yet in spite of her complaints and her apparent ill-humour, she left the comfort of the fire and went down to the stream where she collected some small plants growing at the water's edge. These she pounded between two rocks, and the resulting green pulp she laid softly on the raw skin.

'All the soreness should be gone by morning,' she said.

Then, almost as an afterthought, she tore a broad strip of cloth from the bottom of her cloak, making the garment look more tattered than ever.

'Take it,' she said in a softened tone. 'Roll it up and use it as a pad under your arm.'

Derin took the gift in both hands. For a moment all his earlier doubts about her disappeared. Seeing her standing there in the firelight, a thin scarecrow of a figure, her old face nearly as wrinkled and seamed as the cloak she wore, he felt moved by a mixture of pity and affection.

'Thank you,' he murmured, 'it's very kind . . .'

But she cut him short, a stern edge returning to her voice.

'Don't think I'm doing this just for your sake,' she said. 'I can't afford to leave you behind, nor waste time on your imaginary aches and pains.'

Derin made no reply to her sharp rebuff, and for the remainder of the evening they said little more to each other. Partly that was because they were too tired for conversation. After sharing out and eating some more of the bread, they cut long twiggy branches from the hedge and made makeshift beds beside the fire. These were not very comfortable, but they were preferable to the wet ground. And leaving Craak to stand guard, they both curled up and fell asleep – one or other of them waking at regular intervals throughout the night whenever the growing chill warned them that the fire was burning low.

The second day passed in much the same way as the first, except that by late afternoon they had again reached a more wooded area, the rolling upland country dotted regularly with small groups of trees. That night, as they were sitting before the camp fire, Derin said:

'Surely the woodlands must be quite close by now. When do you think we'll get there?'

Marna was already dozing fitfully, but she jerked awake in response to his question.

'Provided we don't waste too much time in Solwyck,' she replied, 'we should reach the outer limits of the woodlands by tomorrow afternoon.'

'Solwyck?' he said, surprised. 'But that's a village. Why are we going there?'

Marna held both hands out, as if to show him how empty they were.

'We've finished the bread,' she explained, 'and Solwyck is only a few miles from here. We must go there first in order to collect more food.'

'But won't it be dangerous?' he objected. 'Wouldn't it be safer in the cover of the woodlands?'

She sighed impatiently.

'Use your brains, child,' she said. 'What earthly good is safety to us if we're starving? In any case, haven't you realized yet that this whole journey is dangerous? Or is that perhaps what disturbs you?'

He didn't answer. And seeing the hurt and worried expression on his face, she relented and added:

'It needn't be too dangerous, not if we're careful. We can leave Craak outside the village and I can pretend I'm a blind beggar.' She held up the tattered edges of her cloak and laughed. 'At least I'll look the part. With you leading me, I'll appear so old and helpless that no one will give us a second glance.'

And that was precisely what they did. The next morning, an hour or two after sunrise, they left Craak in a huge oak tree that grew beside the road and walked slowly into the village.

As Marna had predicted, they excited no interest in the few passers-by. With Derin holding her hand and Marna shuffling along beside him, her eyes closed and back bent almost double, they were exactly like a blind beggar and her guide; and they reached the centre of the village without once being challenged.

Solwyck was a much bigger place than Sone. The main street was quite wide and strewn with gravel; and in addition to several small shops, it boasted no fewer than three taverns. The most popular of the three was an ugly two-storey building made of wood and roughly cut stone; and outside it, on benches placed along the southern wall, was gathered a group of old men and women obviously enjoying the early spring sunshine.

Marna took in the scene through narrowly opened eyes and murmured softly to Derin:

'We'll stop here. Nobody will notice me amongst so many old people.'

He led her over to an empty space on one of the benches and helped her sit down. Further along the bench an old man with a bald head and a broad, very red face leaned towards her and said in a friendly way:

'Good morning to you, mother. Isn't it good to feel the warm spring sunshine on your face again?'

Instead of answering, she cackled foolishly and rolled her eyes upwards.

'What was that? What was that?' she said in a quavery voice, cupping one hand around her ear.

Derin bent forward and shouted:

'The man's talking to you, Gran. He says he's enjoying the sunshine.'

'Ah, the spring, the spring,' she said, wiping her eyes with the tips of her fingers as though she were crying. 'I didn't think to survive another season. Not with everyone deserting their homes or dying. I kept thinking, I'll be the next one to go. And I will be, too, you'll see.'

'Don't take on, mother,' the red-faced man bawled at her. 'With luck, there're quite a few years left in us yet.'

Marna, her sadness vanishing as quickly as it had appeared, cackled foolishly once again.

'He talks about years,' she quavered. 'I've forgotten about years. One day at a time is what I say, one day at a time.'

As she spoke, she plucked at her cloak, in the manner of one who no longer has anything useful to do with her hands. And even Derin, who knew she was acting, was almost convinced by her transformation.

'Can I get you something to eat, Gran?' he shouted.

'Ah, food and drink,' she mumbled, 'food and drink. That's all there is left. That and a little sleep.'

With shaking hands she fumbled inside her cloak and pulled out a cloth purse. From this, working only by touch, she selected some copper coins and placed them in Derin's palm.

'See what you can get us,' she said, 'and don't let them cheat you. I'll soon be gone from this world, and then you'll have to fend for yourself.'

Leaving her sitting on the bench, he limped into the tavern. A hard-faced woman was standing behind the counter. She was a typical uplander: strongly built, with light brown hair and grey eyes.

'You're a stranger in these parts,' she said suspiciously.

'We're beggar folk,' he explained. 'I travel with my grandmother, who's blind.'

The woman nodded, accepting his story but obviously unmoved by it.

'These are difficult times for everyone,' she said defensively. 'There's barely enough food to go round, and we're certainly in no position to give charity, not even to beggar folk.'

Derin resisted the temptation to make an angry reply.

'I have money,' he said coolly, sliding the coppers across the counter towards her. 'Can you give me some ale and as much food as you think they are worth?'

The woman counted the coppers slowly before dropping them into a drawer below the counter. Then she filled a small jug with ale and placed beside it several hard brown loaves and a good-sized square of cheese. With all these cradled in his left arm, Derin limped back outside.

During his brief absence nothing much seemed to have happened. One other figure, draped in a heavy cloak and hood, had joined the group of old people, but that was all. Marna was sitting exactly as he had left her: leaning back against the sun-warmed stones of the wall, eyes closed, a foolish, vacant smile on her lips.

'Here you are, Gran,' he said loudly, 'drink some of this and we'll be on our way.'

She accepted the jug and took a long grateful drink. But as she handed it back to him, she grasped his wrist and pulled him towards her.

'Stay here a few minutes,' she whispered softly, 'and keep your ears open.'

Reluctantly, he sat down beside her and listened.

The red-faced man who had spoken to them earlier was saying: 'I don't care what you think, it's just a passing phase. Some young hot-head in the Council at Iri-Nan has heard a few ugly rumours, he's panicked, and sent the soldiers up here. That's all there is to it, if you ask me. Give them a few more months of running round the countryside - they'll soon discover they're on a wild-goose chase - and then they'll pack up and go home.'

A tiny old woman answered him. She had small, pinched features and long snow-white hair that was neatly plaited and wound tightly around her head.

'It's all very well calling it a passing phase,' she said, 'but can we dismiss it as easily as that? What about the talk of soldiers being killed no more than a mile from the village? And what persuaded the young men and women to run off as they have - some of them to the mountains, others to Iri-Nan?'

'Do you expect me to believe all that nonsense about soldiers dying?' the red-faced man replied. 'Those are just stories they tell to win us over. They know they'd get little sympathy from us otherwise. And as for the young folk, you mark my words, they'll be back just as soon as all this nonsense blows over.'

Several of the others voiced their approval of these sentiments, and it was just beginning to appear that the discussion was over when a thin, wizened old man rose shakily to his feet. He was so ancient that the flesh seemed to have shrunk away from his bones; and the bones themselves had grown thin and sharp with age, so that now he looked more like a featherless bird than a human being.

'Stuff and nonsense!' he broke out in a high, piping voice. 'Stuff and nonsense, I say.'

'Now don't get yourself all a-tremble,' someone called out, not unkindly.

The old man glared at the speaker, as though daring him at his peril to interrupt again.

'You all know me,' he said, his bird-like head trembling on his thin stalk of a neck. 'And you all know how old I am. A hundred and seven years this equinox.' He paused, allowing the awful fact of his age to have its sobering effect on the audience. 'A hundred and seven,' he repeated, 'and my father nigh on a hundred before me. Between us we've seen and heard more of the goings-on in these parts than all the rest of you put together. And I'm telling you now that there's a deal more than rumours abroad. D'you want to know what I think?' Again he paused, giving his audience time to prepare themselves for what was to come. 'I think the days of the old Kingdom have returned.'

There were murmurs of shocked disbelief from most of his listeners. The tiny white-haired woman said:

'But Wenborn the Wise promised us that those days would never come back again.'

'Aye, he promised us,' the old man piped shrilly, 'but did he have the power to make good that promise? That's what we have to ask ourselves. Think back, every one of you. After the long wars, what happened to the Warden's Staff? The one, we were told, that was made from the topmost branch of the oldest tree in the Grove? Fire, they say, couldn't burn it, nor any axe split it. And what about the Sword of the Kings? The one which was supposed to be older than the human race and was always kept locked up in the Citadel? Hard enough to split rocks, it was.'

'They were both destroyed!' the red-faced man burst out. 'Wenborn the Wise told us he destroyed them.'

'That is indeed what he told us,' the old man replied, his bird-like head trembling more violently than ever, 'but for all his wisdom, did he have the power to carry out such a deed? Look at what's happening around us now, and then answer that question truthfully. No, the Sword and the Staff still exist. And so I tell you again, whether you like it or not, the days of the old Kingdom have returned; and all of you here' – pointing a claw-like finger at everyone present – 'are destined to end your days as I began mine: with the noise of war thundering in your ears.'

As he sat down there was an immediate outburst from most of the other old people, many of them shouting or talking at once. In the midst of all the confusion, Marna rose slowly to her feet.

'Come,' she whispered in Derin's ear, 'time for us to be leaving.'

But before they could steal away, the hard-faced woman who had sold Derin the food came running out into the street.

'Stop all this noise, you old fools!' she shouted harshly. 'What are you trying to do? Bring the soldiers down on us?'

No sooner had she spoken than two soldiers appeared at the far end of the street. Attracted by the shouting, they hurried down towards the tavern. To his dismay, Derin noticed that one of them was the soldier who had confronted them in the inn at Sone. Quickly he hissed a warning to Marna and they both turned away, Derin sliding his crutch round in front of him in the hope that it wouldn't be noticed.

'What's going on here?' the soldier shouted. 'Be silent!'

But the old people, once roused, were not easily quelled. The wizened old man who had spoken of the return of the Kingdom rose shakily to his feet once more and screeched out:

'There they are, the ones who claim to protect us. But I've lived in the shadow of their rule before. Murderers, every one of them!'

The tall, pale-faced soldier drew his sword and pointed it at the old man's quivering neck.

'There'll be no more talk like that,' he said threateningly. 'And that goes for everyone here.'

He ran his eye slowly over the rest of the crowd - and it was then that he spotted Derin and Marna.

'You!' he shouted triumphantly, and leaped towards them.

Derin, in spite of his lame foot, managed somehow to dodge to one side. But Marna was not so lucky. She too tried to dodge, and in doing so stumbled and almost fell. She was given no chance to regain her footing. As she struggled to keep her balance, at the precise moment when she was most helpless, the soldier swung his arm, catching her on the side of the head with the flat of his sword and knocking her senseless to the ground.

There was a shocked silence from the rest of the crowd.

Derin, convinced that she was dead, had drawn his dagger almost without realizing what he was doing.

'You've killed her!' he said in a hoarse, tear-choked voice.

He looked helplessly at the weapon in his hand. He knew, even before he moved, that the short, rusted blade was useless against the soldier's steel sword. Yet still he leaped forward, lunging at the mailed figure before him. It was more an act of desperation than a real attempt to injure his opponent - an act, as he realized afterwards, of sadness and defeat. The soldier, had he wanted to, could have killed him at will. Instead, he merely knocked the flimsy blade from Derin's hand.

Scrambling backwards as quickly as he could, Derin retrieved the dagger and again faced his attacker.

'Listen to me, witch boy,' the soldier said, 'my orders are to take you alive, and if I can, I will. But if you force me to, I'll kill you.'

That brief pause had given Derin time to think. He again looked at the dagger, and with a shrug of resignation pushed it back into its scabbard. The soldier, nodding his approval, lowered his sword slightly. That was what Derin had been waiting for. In one swift movement he swung the crutch upwards and thrust the heavy metal tip straight at his opponent, catching him just below the chin. As the man staggered back, choking and clawing at his throat, Derin whirled the crutch through a full circle and brought it down on the side of his jaw, knocking him unconscious.

The watching crowd gave a murmur of approval. But Derin knew the struggle wasn't over yet: the other soldier still had to be dealt with; and unlike his companion he was completely on his guard. Already he had drawn his sword and begun inching forward.

As quickly as he could, Derin moved further out into the street in order to give himself more space, and then began whirling the crutch above his head. For days he had cursed this cumbersome piece of wood on which he had to rely, but now, at a moment of crisis, it was unaccountably light, moving easily in his hands, the metal tip flashing dangerously in the sunlight as it swung through a tight protective circle at the centre of which Derin stood secure. Never, it seemed, had he felt more confident, more sure of success, and he had actually started to advance on his opponent when he was distracted by someone groaning near by. Briefly he glanced aside, and was delighted to find Marna sitting up, holding both hands to her head.

Yet now it was Derin's turn to be caught unawares. Seizing his opportunity, the soldier charged forward. But before he could take more than a pace or two, there was a muffled thud and he faltered in his stride, a surprised expression on his face. He took two more dragging steps, there was another thud, and his sword slipped from his fingers and fell with a clatter to the gravelled roadway. The soldier now seemed to be pleading with his enemy, his mouth drawn open in a voiceless cry of anguish, his eyes wide with pain and surprise. Derin, mystified, had ceased to whirl the crutch above his head. He stood quite still as the man reached out, touching him lightly on the shoulder, before he stumbled, fell to his knees, and finally, with a soft moan, pitched forward onto the road.

For a moment or two Derin was totally confused. Then, as the first wave of astonishment passed, he saw that there were two arrows protruding from the man's back. It wasn't the first time he had seen such arrows: one identical to these had mortally wounded the soldier whom he and Marna had found lying in the snow.

Without hesitation Derin crouched down and placed his fingers on the man's neck, searching for a pulse. But there was none: he was dead. And there, twenty paces away, standing in the middle of the road, was his assailant: his heavy cloak thrown open, the bow still in his hand, the hood pulled back from his head.

Earlier, when he had emerged from the tavern and noticed this figure sitting at the end of the far bench, Derin had taken him for one of the old people. Now there was no mistaking his identity: the thick woollen muffler around the lower part of the face; the dead eyes staring at him. As on that night at the inn, Derin felt drawn by those eyes, by something hidden within them, which was trying to reach out and probe his mind; some distant force which sought to stir into wakefulness his lost memory. Slowly Derin raised his own eyes towards the muffled face; but before he could meet that dead gaze, Marna called out to him.

'Are you going to stand there all day, boy?' she said irritably. 'Can't you even help an old woman get up?'

She was sitting on the ground beside the wall, and he went over and eased her to her feet. She placed both arms on his shoulders and leaned heavily against him, as though she were still dizzy. But he soon realized that it was merely a trick to get close to him.

'Whatever you do,' she whispered urgently, 'don't look into his eyes.'

Aloud, she went on in a grumbling voice;

'I don't know what the world's coming to. You arrive at a village, looking for a bit of company, and this is the way you're treated. Here we are, innocent people who've never harmed a soul, and yet anyone can happen along and bully and beat us as they please.

Well, we know when we're not wanted. Come, boy, let's get away from here. Let's leave them to their wars or their fights or whatever it is they think they're doing.'

While she was grumbling on, she groped along the wooden bench and gathered up the loaves and cheese they had bought earlier, stuffing them into pockets inside her cloak. Then, watched by the astonished crowd of old people and by the sinister figure of the unknown bowman, she hooked her hand through Derin's arm, and together they hurried away down the sunlit street.

5. The Sword of the Kings

Once outside the village, Marna wanted to leave the road immediately and cut across country.

'It's our only chance of escape,' she said urgently.

But Derin insisted on going back to where they had left Craak.

'He'll be waiting there for us,' he said, 'and it's not much further.'

He was about to hurry on when Marna caught him by the shoulder.

'Think about what you're doing,' she said. 'You're risking our lives for a mere bird.'

'What would you have me do?' he asked. 'Run off and leave him?'

'Would that be so very unusual?' she countered scornfully.

In spite of the danger of their present situation, Derin stopped abruptly and turned to face her.

'I know you don't have a very high opinion of me,' he said, 'but as I've told you before, although I can't alter the past, I can do what I think is right now.'

'Is it right to risk our safety?' she asked coldly.

'But Craak is a part of our safety,' he protested. 'Since coming to us he's warned us of danger, that night in the snow, and he's guarded us while we slept. It would be unfair to desert him now.'

She gave in reluctantly.

'I'll say this in your favour,' she said, 'you've always stood by the creatures of the wood. What I keep asking myself is whether you're capable of standing by your fellow human beings in the same way.'

'If I ever have to,' he said quietly, 'I shall do my best.'

'Oh, your opportunity will come,' she assured him, 'never fear.'

And with a defiant toss of her head she strode on down the road.

They came within sight of the tree about five minutes later. As soon as he saw them, Craak flew to meet them with a cry of welcome; and they immediately turned aside, forcing their way through the prickly hedge which bordered the road. It was fortunate for them that they did: as they stumbled out onto the open pasture-land, they heard the tramp of heavy feet somewhere on the road behind them. And not long afterwards, lying in a shallow ditch which followed the line of the hedge, they watched as a troop of soldiers ran past, the tall, pale-faced soldier at their head.

Not until the sound of footsteps had died away did they dare leave the safety of the ditch. Then, bent almost double, they scurried towards a tree-covered knoll about half a mile distant. From there they could see out over most of the surrounding countryside. Not far away the troop of soldiers had stopped and was breaking up into smaller groups. One of these groups continued on along the road; the others scattered in all directions and began systematically searching any possible hiding places – the thicker parts of the hedge; the groups of trees which dotted the landscape. Clearly it was only a matter of time before they reached the knoll on which Derin and Marna now lay hidden.

'What are we going to do?' Derin asked in a worried voice.

'Somehow,' Marna said thoughtfully, 'we've got to stay out of sight until darkness. After that it will be safe enough to travel in the open.'

Beckoning Derin to follow, she crawled cautiously through the trees and gazed over towards the west. About two or three miles off there was a small slate-roofed farmhouse nestling in a hollow.

'Perhaps that's the answer,' she murmured.

With the knoll between them and the searching soldiers, they hurried down the slope to another group of trees, and then on to another, gradually closing the gap between themselves and the farmhouse. When at last they reached it, after a frantic scramble across the bare hillside above the hollow, they were both breathless, and so concerned with the danger behind them that they were caught completely by surprise as two savage-looking dogs came running around the side of the house.

Only Craak remained in control of the situation. Flying straight towards the dogs, he beat at them with his heavy wings, soaring up out of reach of their snapping jaws only at the last moment; then, having stopped their initial rush, he swept down on them again, pecking at their backs with his sharp black beak. It was a form of attack the dogs had never encountered before, and despite their size they were soon running for cover, letting out long howls of protest as they went.

Yet the noise had alerted whoever was in the house, for now the front door opened and a middle-aged woman looked out.

'Who are you and what do you want?' she called to them.

She had long, greying hair and was dressed in a man's work clothes. Like most of the people they had seen in the course of their journey, she appeared frightened and lonely. In both hands she was gripping a long-handled axe which she held protectively across her body.

'Are you Witch People?' she asked them as they walked towards her along the gravel path.

Instead of answering, Marna raised her hands, the fingers rigid and pointing directly at the woman. It was the same gesture she had made that night at the inn, when she had temporarily placed a spell on the pale-faced soldier. But now Derin stepped quickly in front of her.

'No!' he said, 'leave her!'

'Would you have her betray us?' Marna asked fiercely.

'There are other ways of protecting ourselves,' he replied. And turning to the woman he said gently, 'You have nothing to fear from us. We are running from the soldiers and we need somewhere to hide.'

Slowly the woman lowered the axe.

'I too am no friend of the soldiers,' she said. 'They have taken my husband and my two sons. But it is dangerous to harbour the Witch People.'

'We won't stay long,' Derin said. 'We'll leave as soon as it's dark.'

She hesitated briefly and then opened the door wide.

'I'll give you what help I can,' she said.

Marna ducked quickly through the open doorway, but Derin paused for a moment. Taking Craak from his shoulder, he tossed the bird into the air and watched as it flew to a nearby tree

'Wait,' he called out softly.

And he too entered the house.

The woman led them down a passage to a narrow, flagstoned kitchen at the back. There she pointed to a trapdoor set into the ceiling.

'You can hide in the attic,' she said.

Dragging a deal table into the middle of the room, she placed a box on top of it and a chair on top of that. From the chair it was an easy matter to clamber up through the trapdoor, and within less than a minute Marna and Derin were looking down onto the woman's upturned face.

'Don't make a sound,' she cautioned them. 'I'm going outside to make sure there's no one about.'

They waited in silence. Even with the trapdoor closed it wasn't completely dark up there. Fine strips of sunlight showed between the slates of the roof, creating a strange dusky light in which they could just see each other's faces. They could also see, in the far corner of the attic, a large iron-bound box. It was the only object up there, and after a while Derin crawled silently over to it and raised the lid.

He thought at first it was empty. Then something glinted in the fine dust at the bottom, and he reached in and drew out a sword. It was so old that the cloth binding on the metal sheath dissolved in his hands like wind-blown cobweb, tearing or crumbling into powder the moment he touched it. Carefully, he pulled aside the few remaining shreds and wiped the sheath and hilt free of dust. What he saw made him catch his breath. For the sword was unrusted, unblemished by the years it had lain in the attic: and there, etched clearly on both the sheath and the hilt, was a pattern he was sure he recognized: a tiny sword, drawn in outline, surrounded by a circle of ten stars.

He knew immediately where he had seen such a sign before. On that afternoon when he had woken in the wood, lost and bewildered, the same pattern had been stamped in the snow alongside the footprints of whoever had pursued him. It could have been made by the butt of a spear, by the metal tip of a shepherd's crook, even by a crutch similar to his own. But whatever the cause, one thing was certain: that pattern and the etched design on this ancient sword were identical.

All this flashed through Derin's mind while he was kneeling

before the open box, his back turned to Marna who had remained sitting beside the trapdoor. Now he heard her moving restlessly behind him.

Still with his back to her and forcing himself to sound as calm and natural as possible, he said:

'I've been meaning to ask you: have you ever seen a design or pattern in which a sword is enclosed by a circle of ten stars?'

There was an unusually long pause.

'Why do you ask such a question?' she said at last.

Although he couldn't be sure, Derin thought he could detect a veiled note of alarm in her voice.

'I was just curious,' he said casually. 'I saw exactly that kind of design this morning, hanging on the wall in the tavern, and I wondered whether you might be able to tell me what it meant.'

He heard Marna's shoes scrape the floor as she rose to her feet.

'Yes, I know something about it,' she said guardedly, 'enough to realize that you couldn't possibly have seen it in the tavern.'

He pretended to be surprised by her reply.

'Oh, why is that?' he asked innocently.

'Because what you've described is a sign which hasn't been widely used since the days of the old Kingdom. It was originally employed by the Kings; since then it's been taken over by the Council.'

'Are the members of the Council the only ones who use it?' he asked.

Again she delayed before replying.

'Yes, they're the only ones,' she said quietly, still with a guarded, distrustful undertone to her voice.

Derin again pictured to himself the imprint of the pattern in the snow – and he thought: So it wasn't a soldier. A member of the Council must have followed him into the woods and knocked him out. But why should that have happened to him, a mere boy living on a poor upland farm? Who was he and what had he done that he should merit such attention? He felt a strong urge to put these questions to Marna; but some inner doubt warned him that it would be unwise to do so – and he stifled the temptation. Instead, he asked:

'If the sign dates back to the Kingdom, why did the Council adopt it?'

'I can't be certain of that,' Marna replied. 'There are some who believe that Wenborn the Wise was inspired by the sign itself; that the image of the ten stars enclosing the Sword of power gave him the idea of the controlling Council of ten.'

'But that wasn't its original meaning?'

'No, I don't think so. In the beginning it probably referred to the magical power of the Kings' Sword.'

The magical power of the Kings' Sword! Derin murmured the words softly to himself and looked again at the weapon resting in his hands.

Behind him he heard Marna say:

'Come, boy, enough of these questions. Tell me truly, where did you see this sign?'

Abruptly, Derin turned and held the sword out towards her.

'Here,' he said simply. 'See, it is etched into the metal.'

As he pushed the sword forward he watched her face for a reaction, but, to begin with, her expression remained largely unchanged. If anything, she appeared almost relieved, though that could have been a trick of the light. Only after several seconds did she begin to look alarmed, as if all at once she had noticed some sinister quality about the old weapon. It was a curiously delayed response which Derin didn't quite understand, yet for all that there was no denying the fear which now showed in her eyes.

'Where did you find this?' she asked him in an anxious voice.

'In the box over there.'

'Then put it back,' she urged him, 'quickly!'

'I shall if you tell me why it frightens you,' he said.

She edged nervously away until her back was pressed against one of the supporting roof beams.

'It comes from the days of the old Kingdom,' she said. 'Such things carry with them the evil of the past. It is not good to touch them.'

Had she spoken with conviction, Derin might have accepted her explanation; but there was a hesitant quality about her speech which made him suspect that she was inventing excuses on the spur of the moment.

'Now you're the one who's not telling the truth,' he said. 'There's something else about this sword, isn't there?'

'What else could there be?' she asked sharply.

'Back there in the village,' he said evenly, 'the old man spoke of an ancient Sword of power. The Sword of the Kings, he called it. Could this be what he was referring to?'

'How should I know?' she said, her voice beginning to rise. 'There were many fine swords made in the old times. Why should this one be anything special?'

'Because it bears the sign of power,' he insisted.

'All who supported the King used the sign,' she retorted.

He took a pace towards her.

'If this is not the Sword of the Kings,' he said, 'then why won't you touch it? Go on, take it in your hands.'

She stepped hastily away. Just for a moment she appeared almost to lose her nerve – to become, in truth, the helpless old woman he had led into the village earlier that morning.

'You don't know what you're asking of me!' she said in shrill, quavering tones. 'Why don't you leave me alone?'

'So you admit this is no ordinary sword,' he persisted.

'I admit nothing!' she shrilled back at him.

'Then explain to me why you're so frightened,' he said, pressing her for a definite answer.

She took a deep breath in an unsuccessful attempt to steady herself. Her whole body was now trembling with agitation, her wild grey hair tossing and gleaming in the thin shafts of dusty sunlight which showed through the tiny gaps between the slates of the roof.

'Don't you understand?' she burst out. 'I don't want to know if this is the Sword of the Kings! I fear the very idea. You speak as if to find the Sword would be a wonderful discovery. I tell you it would be a tragedy. Its whereabouts, if they became known, could plunge this region back into a war too terrible to imagine. So be advised: banish all thought of this sword from your mind; cease to think not only about its true identity, but about its very existence. Put it back in the box and pray only that the dust of years will hide it from memory once again.'

'How can I now forget . . . ?' he began, but she interrupted him with some of her old fierceness.

'Are you mad?' she cried. 'Do you willingly choose to burden yourself with a secret knowledge that even the wisest person would shrink from?'

He was about to answer her when they were startled by a sound from below. They both became immediately still - but to Derin's relief it was only the woman of the house calling up to them.

Hastily replacing the sword in the box and closing the lid, he crept back across the attic and raised the trapdoor.

'You're making far too much noise,' the woman warned him. 'Are you trying to get us all killed? I could hear you from the front gate.'

'I'm sorry,' Derin said lamely.

Still frowning with disapproval, the woman climbed up onto the table and handed him a jug of milk and a large round pie. Derin accepted them eagerly, having eaten nothing that day.

'Thank you,' he murmured.

But she placed a cautionary finger on her lips.

'If you want to show your gratitude,' she whispered, 'you can best do it by keeping quiet. The soldiers should be here any minute. They're already searching the bushes and trees on the other side of the slope.'

After she had gone and the trapdoor was closed once again, they shared out the pie and drank thirstily from the jug of milk. Neither of them spoke, but from time to time Derin noticed how Marna glanced anxiously at the box in the corner. Earlier she had denied all knowledge of the sword's true identity; yet now her worried glances suggested otherwise. They seemed to tell him far more clearly than words that he might in fact have stumbled on the Sword of the Kings. The longer he sat there watching her, the more such a possibility grew into a feeling of certainty; and with that feeling of certainty came a strange sense of dread. For he knew that he could not possibly banish all thought of the discovery from his mind as Marna had advised. As yet he had only a hazy idea of the Sword's power; but already his knowledge of it seemed to prey upon his peace of mind, lodging in the forefront of his memory like a guilty secret.

When, a short time later, the dogs began to bark furiously outside, the distraction came almost as a relief from his own brooding thoughts.

'It must be the soldiers,' he whispered to Marna.

She nodded her agreement, her lips set in a grim line, her face unusually tense and still. Derin guessed what was troubling her. It wasn't just the fear of capture; there was another, more disturbing, possibility now. If the soldiers searched the house, they would surely find the box. And after that . . . ? Marna had spoken of a terrible war – as had the old man in the village. Derin wasn't sure why that should be so; yet the vision which their words conjured in his mind filled him with foreboding.

Again he was distracted from such thoughts, this time by heavy footsteps on the gravel path. He heard the woman go to the door and there was a murmur of voices. He couldn't make out what was being said at first – not until the woman suddenly raised her voice in protest.

'What do you want to come in for?' she cried out. 'I've told you, there's nobody here.'

'Get out of our way!' a voice replied roughly.

Now the footsteps could be heard in the house itself. There was a noise of furniture being moved, of cupboards being searched; finally one of the soldiers lumbered into the kitchen. Derin and Marna looked at each other in the half-light, neither of them daring to move – hardly daring even to breathe as they listened to the movements below them. Something was knocked over with a crash; a door was banged open; then there was a tinkle of glass, the popping of a cork, and the gurgle of someone drinking. Immediately all the tension disappeared from Marna's face, and her lips slowly parted in a smile.

'Hey, lads,' the soldier called out. 'Look what I've found here: a cupboard full of cider.'

More soldiers tramped heavily into the kitchen. Chairs were scraped back, followed by the sound of cider being poured into mugs.

'Ah, this is more like it,' someone said.

'Better by far than legging it across this god-forsaken country.'

Cautiously, Derin raised the trapdoor a fraction and put his eye to the crack. Three rough-looking soldiers, unwashed and unshaven, were seated around the table below him. They all had full mugs of cider in front of them, and in the middle of the table stood a cluster of unopened bottles.

'What about some food?' one of the soldiers shouted, and banged his mug down heavily, spilling cider across the scrubbed table-top.

Derin lowered the trapdoor and leaned back, making himself as comfortable as possible. The soldiers were clearly preparing for a long drinking session, and many hours would have to pass before he and Marna could hope to escape. He glanced over at his companion and saw with surprise that she had already settled herself against one of the roof beams and fallen asleep. It seemed incredible to him that she could sleep in such a situation. But as the day wore on he too began to doze. Throughout the afternoon he woke up every half hour or so, disturbed by the shouting or raucous singing from below. But just before dusk, having grown used to the constant noise, he fell at last into a deep sleep.

He was woken by Marna shortly before midnight. The singing had stopped and all about them the house felt unnaturally still.

'We must leave while we have the chance,' she whispered to him.

They opened the trapdoor and looked down onto the candle-lit kitchen. Two of the soldiers were sprawled back in their chairs; the third had fallen forward, his forehead resting on the table. All three were snoring drunkenly. The grey-haired woman, tired and harassed, was standing against the far wall. She had obviously been waiting for Derin and Marna to appear, because she immediately stood up, nodding her approval. As silently as possible, she cleared a space amongst the litter of mugs and bottles and placed a box and chair on the table - steadying them with both hands as Marna climbed slowly down.

Derin followed her. But before he reached the floor, the soldier who was lying slumped over the table, probably disturbed by some slight noise, suddenly raised his head and stared directly at him with bloodshot eyes. Derin froze exactly where he was - one hand ready to reach for his dagger, the other tightening on the stout wood of his crutch. Neither he nor the soldier moved for a moment. Derin could see the man struggling to understand what was happening before his very eyes, his mind groping through a fog of drunkenness. Fortunately, the effort was too much for him: his eyes glazed over and he flopped forward once again, his head striking the table with a thump.

'Be quick!' the woman whispered, and led them through the house to the front door.

As Derin stepped out into the cold night air, there was a flurry of wings in the darkness and Craak landed lightly on his shoulder.

'Craak,' the bird said softly, as though in welcome, and nuzzled its beak into his hair.

The woman had drawn the door closed behind them so that no sound of their departure should reach the kitchen.

'You must make haste and get as far away as possible,' she said. 'If I can, I'll keep the soldiers here until dawn.'

Marna, her cloak wrapped tightly about her to keep out the cold and damp, gazed intently at the woman in the dim starlight.

'Almost everyone else we've met has been frightened or at least wary of us,' she said. 'You alone have shown us kindness ...' She seemed to hesitate before adding: '... more kindness than you will perhaps ever know. I thank you for it sincerely.'

And she bowed low to show her gratitude.

As she straightened up, the woman touched her lightly on the shoulder. It was, Derin thought, a peculiarly loving gesture.

'When my sons were both babies,' she said, 'they caught the red fever. All around here children were dying. But mine were saved by the Witch People. So you see, it is I who must thank you. I have never forgotten those times. I know that when Witch People enter a house, they bring with them a blessing.'

At the sound of the word blessing, Marna frowned and glanced quickly at Derin. As their eyes met, she turned slowly away and looked deliberately at the roof of the house. Even in the poor light he could see that her face was deeply troubled once more, as it had been earlier when they had huddled together in the attic. Following her gaze, he too sought out the black outline of the roof beneath which, as he was only too fully aware, the box with its secret burden lay hidden.

Beside him he heard Marna murmur softly:

'I fear we may have brought a curse upon you, and yet you call our coming here a blessing. Ah, I hope that what you say proves to be true. With all my heart I wish it.'

And lowering her head, as though in grief, she walked slowly away into the darkness.

6. The Cave of Obin

It was a dark windy night, and having set out so late they couldn't afford to stop and rest. Soon after they left the farmhouse, Derin said:

'Do you think we can reach the woodlands by morning?'

Marna shook her head.

'I don't think so; but we should be able to get quite close.'

They walked on as quickly as they could, avoiding roads, striking straight across country - two small figures stealing away through the protective darkness. As the night wore on the wind rose, whipping at their hair and clothes, moaning through the branches of the trees that crowned the hilltops or nestled in the hollows. Above their heads the clouds swirled angrily across the sky, blotting out the stars; stray showers slanted down on them, the wind-driven drops of water stinging their cheeks.

Throughout the night they saw no one - though in such thick darkness they could have passed within a dozen paces of a soldier and still escaped detection. In many respects the conditions could not have been better for them; for although they were cold and wet, there was little chance of their being taken. Yet in spite of that Marna did not appear to be happy.

She paused only once, at the top of a steep rise, her head raised as though she were listening, her hair streaming in the wind.

'What's the matter?' Derin asked her.

'I don't like it,' she said uneasily. 'At this time of year the wind should be coming from the south, bringing warm air from across the plains. But it isn't. Do you feel that chill in the air? That's because it's blowing from the eastern mountains, from the stronghold of the Grove.'

'Why should that worry us?' he said. 'We're safe for the time being.'

'Safe, d'you say?' she replied doubtfully. 'Aye, maybe so. Just the same, I'd be happier with a warm wind blowing in my face.'

Soon after that the land began to slope away beneath their feet and they dropped steadily down, leaving the harsher upland country behind them. When dawn finally broke they were passing through gentle pasture-lands; and there, no more than three miles distant, was the beginning of the woodlands. Neither of them suggested stopping now; they knew that in just one more hour they would reach the security of the trees. None the less, Marna looked keenly from side to side, on the lookout for any sign of movement.

'If the soldiers are going to ambush us anywhere,' she said grimly, 'this will be the place.'

Yet the minutes passed and nothing happened. The three miles shrank to one; and soon the trees were less than a hundred paces away.

'We've done it!' Derin said, his face flushed with success.

But no sooner had he spoken than a tall, helmeted soldier stepped out from the trees and walked towards them. Both Marna and Derin stopped in their tracks. There was no point in running. The man was armed with a throwing axe and it was clear from the look on his face that he was prepared to use it if they tried to escape. Derin took a firm hold of his crutch, ready to defend himself, though he was not quite sure what he could do against the axe. Marna, beside him, laid a hand on his shoulder.

'Leave this to me,' she said softly.

Hunching her shoulders and bending over, she again became the frail old woman he had led into the village. With faltering steps she hobbled to meet the advancing soldier. But he had obviously heard of her powers because he raised the axe threateningly above his head and called out:

'Stay where you are, witch!'

That command might almost have been a secret signal, because now another figure stepped out from the cover of the trees, behind the soldier. He was dressed in a cloak and hood and the whole of the lower part of his face was hidden in a thick woollen muffler. In his hands were a bow and arrow, the bow already half bent as he raised it and took aim.

From where Derin stood, it appeared that Marna was the bowman's target.

'Look out!' he yelled.

But even before Marna could throw herself to the ground, Derin realized his mistake. There was a sharp twang as the bow-string was released, and the soldier lurched to one side and fell face down onto the ground, the flight of an arrow protruding from the small of his back.

With a cry of concern, Derin sprang forward; but Marna had already risen nimbly to her feet and now stood barring his way.

'Don't interfere with them!' she shouted, grasping him firmly by the shoulders. 'Let them fight their war alone. It's no business of ours.'

'How can you say that?' he protested. 'The man may be dying!'

'And what help can you give him?' she answered angrily. 'Do you think you can stop this war with your bare hands and your fine feelings? Don't you see, you'll only get yourself killed as well.'

'No!' he burst out. 'You're wrong! We have to help him!'

With a violent shrug of his shoulders he tore himself free and pushed past her - only to find himself confronted by the bowman. He had not expected the man to be so close, and with a start he remembered Marna's warning never to look into his eyes. But already it was too late. Those dead eyes, blank and curiously sightless, had riveted themselves upon his face. Unable to resist, he stared into them, sensing rather than actually seeing the unknown presence which lurked in their depths.

'No,' he whispered, 'no . . .'

It was a feeble and useless protest. He stood there, powerless to move, as some invisible force flowed into his mind, searching out the darkest, remotest corners of his memory. He saw in a series of vivid flashbacks his own journey across the uplands: he and Marna wading through the melting snow; both of them asleep beside the tall hedge, Craak standing guard above them; their entrance into the village of Solwyck. Each of these images darted across his inner vision and was gone, as though discarded by some unseen hand. And then all at once he was back in the farmhouse attic, kneeling before the open box. Once again he reached inside and drew out the sword, holding it in one hand while with the other he wiped away the dust and the remnants of cloth. Cradling it now in both hands, almost reverently, he murmured something to himself. No sound could be heard, but he could read the words on his own lips quite easily: 'The magical power of the Kings' Sword.' As these words formed themselves in his mind, something inside him, something entirely separate from himself, seemed to exult, to croon with delight. Who or what that something was he had no idea; nor did he have a chance of finding out. As abruptly as he had left it, so now he found himself back in the present. Craak was squawking loudly, his wings beating in his face; and Marna, her fingernails digging into the flesh of his arm, was trying to pull him towards the line of trees.

'You fool!' she was shouting. 'I told you not to look at him!'

Confused, feeling strangely empty and drained, Derin continued to stare at the bowman.

'Who are you? What do you want?' he asked fearfully.

For the first and only time the man spoke to him. His voice, dry and hollow, almost ghostly in its effect, was oddly in keeping with his dead, lustreless eyes.

'I bring you a message,' he said in cold, distant tones, the words slightly muffled by the woollen mask. 'If ever you are in need of a refuge, you will find one in the holy precincts of the mountain Grove.'

The bowman raised his arm and pointed to the east. It was the very last gesture he ever made. Unnoticed by all of them, the mortally wounded soldier had managed to clamber to his feet. Blood frothed at his lips and his breath came in searing gasps. On his face was the haggard look of one close to death. Yet for all that he continued to clutch the axe with both trembling hands. Swaying from side to side, he drew the axe back over his head and with the last of his strength hurled it at his enemy. It was an effort that cost him his life; but the axe, driven by the force of desperation, found its mark. Passing beneath the bowman's outstretched arm, it bit through the cloth of his cloak and buried itself in his side.

The weight of the blow made the bowman stagger sideways and sink to his knees. He didn't try to get up; nor did he show any surprise. His eyes, dull and blank, continued to stare incuriously before him as though nothing had happened. Slowly, without even a sigh or murmur of protest, he toppled forward and rolled onto his back. As he did so, his cloak fell open, revealing a body and limbs so thin that they were more like the bones of a skeleton than the flesh and blood of a living man. His woollen muffler had also slipped aside, showing the lower part of his face. Again it seemed inconceivable that it could belong to a live human being, presenting to Derin's horrified gaze the image of a death's-head. The nose was shrunken; the mouth withered; the skin like thin yellow parchment, dry and cracked, stretched over the jutting bones of jaw and skull.

'He's dead!' Derin burst out in horror. 'He's been dead all along!'

'No, not dead, child,' Marna said quietly, 'merely dying slowly, the life withering away inside him.'

'But how ...?' Derin began.

He didn't finish. The bowman's staring eyes, which had remained open until then, began to flicker closed.

'Quick!' Marna hissed urgently. 'It is dangerous to remain here!'

Grasping Derin's hand, she began to drag him towards the trees. But before they could take more than a pace or two, the man's eyes had closed in death. And at that moment, as the bony jaws gaped open, a black cloud of vapour issued from the mouth and nostrils. It hovered above the skeletal face only for a second or two - until, caught by a strong gust of wind, it moved with menacing speed straight towards Derin and Marna.

What happened next was so rapid and confused that Derin found it difficult to follow, least of all to understand. Craak leaped from his shoulder and, with a ringing cry, flew directly at the advancing cloud. For a short time the bird and the sinuous wraith of vapour tussled together in mid air, while the wind, strengthening from the east, rose to a shrieking gale. Then, overcome either by the wind or by some more sinister force, Craak was tossed into the air and sent tumbling high above the open pasture-land. Instantly, Marna moved forward to take Craak's place. With fingers outstretched, she mumbled words which the wind caught and tore at, but could not entirely drown out. For a brief space the black cloud hovered in front of her, held there by whatever spell she had woven. But then she too was buffeted aside; and Derin was left standing alone, the wind jerking at his hair and clothes, the writhing black cloud bearing down on him. He had no opportunity to think, to dodge, to run. Almost as a reflex action, he raised and whirled his crutch, the heavy metal tip cutting a circle through the air. And to his astonishment it was that circle which seemed to protect him. Like a ring of steel, it stopped the forward rush of the cloud and stilled even the howling gale.

There was a lull in which everything was so quiet that he could hear his own laboured breathing and the soft groans made by Marna as she struggled to her feet. He waited, the seconds slowly passing; and when he was quite sure that all was still, he took the crutch in his right hand and drove the metal tip firmly down onto the ground. He had no clear idea of why he did that – he sensed only that it was the right thing to do – but the effect was immediate. The dark, menacing vapour began to coil rapidly in upon itself, swirling and gyrating in an agony of aimless movement. Gradually it rose higher and higher until, with what sounded like a thwarted cry, it fled towards the east; and as it disappeared from view, so the warm wind which Marna had wished for earlier began to blow gently from the south.

Still feeling dazed by what had taken place, Derin stared at the ground between his feet. There in the soft earth was the patterned imprint of the tip of his crutch: a ten-pointed star enclosed by a circle.

He glanced up, a questioning look in his eyes, and saw Marna calmly smoothing back her wild grey hair.

'What was it?' he asked her softly.

'You have done well,' was all she said, and she brushed his cheek fondly with the knuckles of her hand.

Before he could repeat his question there was a cry from just above his head and Craak again settled onto his shoulder.

'Is he all right?' Marna asked.

Derin inspected his ruffled flight-feathers.

'He seems to be fine,' he replied.

'Then we must be on our way,' she declared. 'It's dangerous to linger out here in the open.'

'But what about these?' Derin asked, indicating the dead soldier and bowman. 'Shouldn't we bury them?'

Marna shook her head sadly.

'I fear we will see more like this in the miles ahead,' she replied.

'If we stop to bury them all, we will never complete our mission, which is to rescue your father. In any case, other soldiers will come searching for their comrade. They can see to the bodies. Let those who do the killing also do the burying. Better for us if we take no part in their war.'

When Derin still hesitated, she hooked her arm through his.

'Come, child,' she said, 'in these matters at least, you can trust me.'

And she led him across the short stretch of open pasture towards the edge of the woodlands.

It was still too early in the year for the woods to be in leaf, even at that lower altitude, but the first signs of spring growth could be seen on every hand. The buds on the trees and bushes were bursting open, revealing their bright green hearts; tiny coils of fern were pushing up through the dry fronds and dead stalks; and soft, furry shoots were appearing on the hoops of bramble. Walking along the narrow paths between the trees, Derin soon lost his feelings of horror at the grisly scene he had just witnessed. Yet that didn't diminish his desire to understand what had happened; and at the first opportunity, when they stopped for a meal beside a shallow stream, he said to Marna:

'Back there, why did the bowman defend us against the soldier?'

'Perhaps he didn't simply defend us,' she replied shortly. 'Perhaps he was intent on killing the soldier anyway.'

'But then why didn't he kill us?'

Marna washed her hands in the bubbling waters of the stream, clearly unwilling to answer him. Taking out one of the loaves she carried, she broke it into two equal portions and added a piece of cheese to each. She handed one of the portions to Derin.

'Eat,' she said.

He accepted the food in both hands.

'Why won't you tell me what you know?' he asked resentfully.

'What I know?' she said, raising her eyebrows in mock surprise. 'I've already told you, I know very little for certain.'

'But you suspect a great deal,' he insisted.

'Ah, yes,' she said with a sigh, 'I suspect more and more each day. But I thought we'd agreed that I shouldn't voice my suspicions, not until I'm sure about them.'

'That was days ago!' he said angrily. 'How long do you expect me to take your silence on trust?'

Before replying, she peered up at the overcast sky through the canopy of almost leafless branches. A bright spot in the cloud told her where the sun was.

'It's just past midday,' she said. 'We haven't far to go now. We should reach our immediate destination before nightfall. Be patient a little longer. Soon, perhaps this very night, I'll be able to tell you more.'

'But where are we making for?' he asked. 'You haven't even told me that.'

'We are going to visit a friend ...' she began - and corrected herself, a trace of sadness in her voice: 'No, better to say the home of a friend.'

She would tell him no more than that, and after their frugal meal they set out once again. Marna led the way, remaining close to the stream, following it towards its source in a distant range of hills which Derin occasionally glimpsed through the trees. Despite his resentment at being told so little, he felt oddly contented at finding himself in the woodlands. There was something almost familiar about it: the protective latticework of branches above his head; the springy feel of the leaf mould beneath his feet; the velvety sheen of moss clinging to the bark of the trees. He couldn't escape the feeling that he had seen it all before, that he knew it intimately. He puzzled over this for some time - until he remembered something Marna had said to him: how he had always brought home wild creatures from the small upland wood that bordered their farm. Yes, he told himself, that was the explanation: since early childhood he had spent most of the daylight hours accustoming himself to similar surroundings.

Limping along behind Marna, he tried to recall those childhood experiences. But no matter how hard he concentrated, he could not penetrate the silence and darkness which obscured his memory of the past. Always he was forced back to his cold and painful awakening in the snow; almost everything before that remained a total blank. The one vivid image he retained of his father had come to him mainly through a dream - the dream he had had the night before he and Marna left the burned-out farmhouse, when his father had stopped in the snow and turned towards him, appealing to him to follow. That image, more than any other, kept returning to him, and he clung to it as the one sure point in the midst of all the doubt which now beset him.

He was distracted from his own thoughts by Craak, who had begun to move restlessly on his shoulder. With some surprise, he noticed that the afternoon was well advanced. The hills, which had been so far off, now rose steeply before him; and the stream had become a small sparkling rill. A short way ahead Marna had stopped and was motioning for him to move up quietly beside her.

'From this point on,' she whispered, 'we must take extra care.'

'But I thought we were going to see a friend,' he said.

'That's true,' she replied, 'but someone may have been here before us.'

One behind the other, crouched low, they left the path and moved cautiously towards the face of the hillside. Dusk was almost upon them when they reached it. From the cover of a sprawling holly bush they peered across an open, rock-strewn slope towards the dark mouth of a cave.

'It looks deserted to me,' Derin whispered.

Marna nodded, her face unexpectedly drawn and worried.

'That is partly what I dreaded,' she said softly.

She straightened up - and at that moment Craak left Derin's shoulder and flew low across the slope towards the cave mouth. Before reaching it, he veered aside and landed on an upright slab of rock which stood at the head of a narrow mound of earth. Together, Marna and Derin left the cover of the holly bush and followed him; but the bird did not turn to them as Derin expected, though he was obviously disturbed by something, for he hopped restlessly from one foot to the other, continually moving his head from side to side, his bright round eyes fixed on the mound beneath him.

'What do you think is troubling Craak?' Derin asked.

Marna made a sobbing noise and brushed a hand across her face.

'The bird is mourning,' she said quietly.

She raised a ragged corner of her cloak and wiped tears from her eyes. Then, lowering herself to her knees, she bent forward and touched her forehead to the earth, her long grey hair covering the foot of the mound.

Derin did not disturb her until she had risen to her feet. Her eyes, which had often glanced at him so fiercely, were now red-rimmed and swollen.

'Is somebody you know buried here?' Derin asked in an awed whisper.

'Yes, I knew him,' she replied in a choked, uncertain voice. 'He was Craak's master - and mine too when I was a young girl.'

'So this is why Craak came to us?' Derin said.

'Yes,' she murmured. 'I feared exactly this when I first saw the bird. But I had to make sure. Murder isn't a thing to be guessed at.'

'Murder!' Derin answered in astonishment. 'If he was once your master, then he must have been very old. Why couldn't he have died of old age?'

'Because if that had happened, Craak would have remained here. This is his place. He would have waited for ...'

She hesitated, and Derin asked quickly:

'Who would he have waited for?'

Marna took a deep breath and sighed.

'Let me explain,' she said. 'Do you remember what I told you about the Circle of ten? How it replaced the Warden of the Grove? And how the Council of ten took over the powers of the King?'

'Yes, I remember,' Derin answered. 'You said the tenth member of the Circle or Council is unknown to the others, living elsewhere, in secret.'

'That is so,' Marna said. 'Well, now I can tell you this: the old man who lies dead beneath this mound was called Obin, and he was the tenth member of the Circle of the Grove.'

'You mean the secret one?' Derin asked.

'Aye, the secret one,' she affirmed. 'Only a few of the Witch People knew his true identity - though for miles around he was famed for his wisdom and great powers. He has lived here all his life, and Craak with him.'

'But you still haven't explained why you think he was murdered,' Derin said. 'Couldn't you be mistaken?'

'There is no mistake,' Marna answered sadly. 'Had Obin died

peacefully, Craak would have waited here for his successor to arrive – because somewhere in the land there is already a new tenth member of the Circle and in time he too will come here. Only violence could have driven Craak away. Look at the bird now: he is troubled still by what he witnessed. No, Obin was killed; and Craak fled in terror. Of that I'm sure.'

'But what reason would anyone have for killing a peaceful old man?' Derin objected. 'It would be an act of madness.'

'An act of madness, maybe,' she conceded, 'yet perhaps not wholly without reason.'

'I don't follow what you mean,' Derin admitted.

'Then let me show you,' she said grimly, and led him up the slope.

The interior of the cave was unexpectedly neat and tidy: a well-tended rush bed in one corner; banks of shelves filled with small jars and bundles of herbs lining most of the side walls; hessian curtains covering two doorways that led into neighbouring caves; and in the middle of the floor, below a small opening in the roof, an iron grate in which wood and moss had been carefully laid for a fire. In the deepening twilight, Marna strode over to the grate and lit the fire with the tinderbox she always carried. When it was burning well, she took a torch of twisted reeds from one of the shelves, lit it at the fire, and walked deeper into the cave. At the far end was a tall slab of rock.

'Stand back, boy,' she said quietly.

And reaching out with one hand, she mumbled some words to herself.

'Now move the rock away,' she instructed him.

He put his shoulder to it, doubtful whether he possessed sufficient strength; but it felt surprisingly light, sliding easily aside.

Behind it was a small alcove about the size of a cupboard. With the torch held high above her head, Marna looked inside, Derin peering from beneath her arm. Neither of them moved for a moment, though Derin could see at a glance that the alcove was empty.

'Gone!' Marna said at last.

Her voice, normally so firm, now sounded hollow and stricken.

'What was in there?' Derin asked her.

'Gone!' she said again, as though she hadn't heard him, 'the ancient Staff of the Grove, gone!' And then all at once she screeched out, 'A curse upon the thief! May it burn out his eyes and send him stumbling into darkness!' Her voice rose higher, to a howl of desperate rage: 'May its terrible power turn his brain into dust, his body into ashes! May he . . . !'

She broke off, choking with rage, her hands trembling so violently that she actually dropped the torch. Derin stooped to retrieve it, and became aware of a movement somewhere behind him. He turned quickly to see a dim figure standing just inside the entrance of the cave, and heard a voice saying accusingly:

'Who are you, that you dare to desecrate the cave of Obin?'

7. The Thief

At the sound of the voice, Marna whirled around and glared at the shadowy entrance of the cave.

'I'm no thief, if that's what you mean!' she said angrily. 'I am Marna, the Witch of Sone. I have as much right as anyone to be here; and so does the boy, Derin, who travels with me.'

The unknown figure now stepped forward into the firelight. She was a young girl, no more than a year or two older than Derin, with long black hair and dark eyes. Like Marna, she wore a dress of woven black wool.

'Ah yes,' she said, apparently satisfied, 'I've heard Obin speak of you.'

'You knew Obin?' Marna asked sharply.

'He was my great-grandfather,' the girl replied.

'And you lived here with him?'

'Yes.'

'Then you know how he died?'

The girl winced slightly, as though at some painful recollection.

'I was here,' she said simply.

Derin saw an eager gleam appear in the old woman's eyes.

'Tell me, child,' she said with an unexpected show of friendliness, 'what is your name?'

As she spoke, she advanced slowly down the cave, until she was only a pace or two from the girl.

'I am called Asti,' she replied.

'That is a good name,' Marna said admiringly.

She murmured the name several times and then raised her hands towards the girl's face.

'Asti,' she said in a low voice, 'I conjure you to tell ...'

But before she could finish, the girl lifted a short wooden stick she was carrying and held it slantwise across her face.

'You cannot force me to speak,' she said quietly. 'I too am of the Witch People.'

Immediately, all trace of friendliness left Marna's face.

'Then honour your kinship!' she shouted. 'Speak, girl! Tell me how the alcove comes to be empty.'

Again her hands twitched and moved upwards; and again the girl raised the stick. But this time Derin limped forward and stepped between them.

'Enough of this,' he said firmly. And then to Marna, 'You can't force everyone to do as you want. That makes you as bad as the soldiers.'

Marna, her eyebrows drawn together in a bitter frown, seemed about to make some angry reply; but at the last moment she shrugged helplessly and walked slowly over to the rush bed, where she sat down with a weary sigh.

'He's right,' Asti said gently. 'I'll tell you what I know without any threats. But you both look tired. Let us eat something first.'

At the mention of how tired they looked, Derin felt the weariness of the past eighteen hours settle heavily upon him. Marna also appeared deeply fatigued; and she made no further protest as Asti disappeared into one of the adjoining caves and returned bearing an iron pot which she heated over the open fire. When at last Derin was handed a brimming bowl of stew, he accepted it gratefully, for it was the first hot food he had had for days. Even Marna seemed mellowed by the appetizing smell, and she proceeded to eat her portion with astonishing speed.

The meal over, Derin would have liked nothing better than to curl up beside the fire. But Marna, despite the lines of fatigue on her face, looked questioningly across at Asti.

'Well, girl,' she said sternly, 'I'm waiting.'

Asti settled herself on a low stool and carefully stirred the glowing coals of the fire.

'I will tell you what I can,' she said. 'For most of my life I've lived here with Obin. I was sent here when I was only seven, as soon as it was discovered that I was of the Witch People. Obin looked after me, taught me his secrets, acted like a father ...'

'Yes, yes,' Marna broke in impatiently, 'but come to the point. How is it that the alcove is empty?'

'Hear me out,' Asti answered. 'The Staff wasn't stolen by some stray thief - you know that would have been impossible. Its disappearance has a history of its own and I must tell it in my own way.'

'Oh, very well,' Marna grumbled.

Asti drew closer to the fire.

'About four years ago,' she went on, 'a young man called Krob came here and asked Obin if he would teach him the ways of the Witch People. At first Obin refused. Although he recognized that Krob possessed great natural power, he distrusted his proud look. He told him he couldn't teach him humility, which was the greatest of gifts, and that without it none of his lessons was of any use. But instead of leaving, Krob sat down on the slope and waited. He didn't eat or drink or sleep, remaining there even throughout the cold nights. On the third day Obin told him that what he was doing was a sign not of humility but of pride. But it made no difference to Krob: he stayed exactly where he was, waiting for Obin to relent and accept him. On the fourth day I disobeyed Obin and put food and water before him. He didn't touch it. By then his tongue was swollen and his eyes were red and sore. In all that time he hadn't spoken a word; and soon afterwards he fainted with exhaustion.

'I found him like that on the fifth day, and Obin and I carried him in here and nursed him back to health. As soon as he could stand, he again asked Obin to accept him as an apprentice, but still Obin refused. So Krob staggered out onto the slope once more and sat down to wait - though now he looked so unwell that I pleaded with Obin to change his mind.'

'And did he?' Marna asked.

'He gave me a curious answer,' Asti replied. 'He said that I had more compassion than wisdom, for it was foolish to feel sorry for one who knew nothing of pity. And then he added that sometimes it was better to be foolish than to be harshly wise.'

'So he relented and accepted him,' Marna murmured.

'Yes, he allowed him to build a small hut down there at the bottom of the slope, and early each morning he taught both of us and gave us our tasks for the day. That was in the beginning. But soon Krob left me far behind. He learned so quickly; he seemed to forget nothing. And his power with the rowan staff surpassed anything I've ever heard of.'

'How long did he stay here?' Marna asked.

'For three years.'

'That's a long time,' Marna said thoughtfully. 'You must have got to know him well. What was he like?'

'That's the odd thing: in all that time I never came to understand what he was really like. If there were things to be done, he always did them quickly and willingly. And if you gave him anything or helped him in any way, he always thanked you politely. Yet he never revealed what he felt; he never showed you what was going on inside him. I remember once, when I asked Obin whether Krob could come and live here in the cave with us, Obin answered, "He can leave his lonely hut and share this cave only when his heart melts within him." I think that's what worried us most - his coldness. He didn't seem to have emotions like other people. He was just a mind that learned and observed.'

She paused, a distant, uneasy expression on her young face.

'Why did he leave?' Marna asked, gently prompting her.

'In the last few months of his stay here, he began to take more and more notice of the alcove. I didn't even know there was an alcove then, but during our lessons in the morning I would see his eyes continually straying towards the far end of the cave. And one afternoon, when I came in unexpectedly, I found him standing in front of the slab of rock.'

'What was he doing?' Marna asked.

'He was trying to move it - I'm sure of that now. His eyes were closed and he was tapping his rowan staff gently on the upper part of the rock. But of course it wouldn't budge.'

Marna glanced across at Derin who was listening attentively.

'What Asti means,' Marna explained to him, 'is that the rock wasn't just held in place by a spell as it is now. It was also held there by the power of Obin himself. He stood between the rock and any intruder. The rock could not be moved while he lived.'

Asti nodded her head sadly.

'That is so,' she said, 'though Krob didn't realize it at the time. He thought that all he had to do was break the binding spell. One day, while he was trying to do that, Obin discovered him here. I'd never seen Obin so angry before. He told Krob that he'd obviously learned nothing during the years of his apprenticeship and that he would waste no more time on him. The following morning he sent him away, instructing him to go and work amongst the poor and to return only when he had lost his love of power and discovered the true aims of the Witch People.'

'And did he return?' Derin asked.

'Yes, a few months later. Obin must have guessed what might happen, because one night he told me about the alcove and the Warden's ancient Staff hidden inside it. He said that if any accident befell him, then I must take his place and bind my life to the closed rock until another member of the Circle arrived here. I promised him I would, but unfortunately I never got the chance. The next day I went out into the woodlands to gather herbs, and when I returned I found –' she faltered only for a moment '– I found Obin dead and the alcove empty.'

'But how do you know that Krob was the culprit?' Derin objected.

'Because it was his staff which struck down Obin. I found it here on the floor. He had cast it aside after stealing the Warden's Staff.'

She was interrupted by a stifled groan from Marna. They both looked at the old woman who was sitting bent over, her face in her hands.

'It is as I've feared,' she moaned, 'the old conflicts are come back to plague us.' With an effort she straightened up and returned Derin's gaze. 'Listen to me, boy!' she said urgently. 'We have no time to lose. I asked you to trust me until certain things became clearer. Well, I'm no longer in any doubt. I tell you now: the plains are doomed, as is everyone in them. If we are to save your father, we must act quickly. For unless we find him soon and help him to escape, he too will perish.'

Involuntarily, Derin had risen to his feet, remembering again the way his father had appealed to him in the dream. He wanted to answer that appeal, but he also felt slightly confused by what Marna had just said.

'I'm not sure if I understand,' he said hesitantly.

'What's the matter with you, boy?' Marna almost shouted at him. 'Can't you use your brains? Didn't you hear the old man in the village of Solwyck? I thought what he said was plain enough!'

'But you told me that war was impossible,' Derin protested, 'that after what Wenborn the Wise had done ...'

Marna silenced him with a wave of her hand.

'I also mentioned other disturbing fears that plagued me,' she said more quietly, 'fears I was unwilling to put into words lest they grow into monsters of reality. You see, what the old man said in Solwyck is true. Wenborn, for all his wisdom, could not destroy the two most ancient symbols of power: the Warden's magical Staff and the Sword of the Kings. Yet he knew that while they existed there could be no guarantee of peace. Either object, in the wrong hands, could override the decisions and desires of a hundred Councils or Circles. For instance, had I evil intent in my heart and the sacred Staff in my grasp, there is no one who could stand against me. Wenborn knew that as well as anyone. And as he couldn't destroy these fearful objects, he took the only other path open to him: he hid them where he hoped they would never be discovered. The Staff, I know, was locked away in that alcove; and its guardian was the pure, uncorrupted heart of Obin.'

'And that is the Staff that has been stolen by Krob,' Asti added.

Marna wagged her head vigorously.

'He is now in the mountains,' she said, 'where he will have ousted the elders of the Circle and taken over the sacred Grove. From there he is attracting men and women to his banner, preparing to declare war on the plains.'

'Then the real war hasn't yet begun?' Derin queried.

'No, not yet, but it will begin soon, very soon. That is why the soldiers are everywhere. They have been sent out by the Council in an attempt to secure the uplands against attack. But it will do no good. Already Krob has started to probe into the territory of his enemies. The man with dead eyes, who was following us, is just one of his outriders. Their task is to recruit men for the growing armies of the Grove, to harry the soldiers, and also to spy out the...'

'They are Krob's spies?' Derin broke in sharply, and again lurched hastily to his feet.

'Yes, they are poor creatures taken over by him. It's a practice which he must have learned from the days of the old Kingdom. The self is almost extinguished inside such men; they are directed wholly by the power of the Staff. It is that power which we witnessed this morning, in the black vapour that rose from the bowman's mouth and nostrils. It was leaving his dead body, seeking some other victim to inhabit. That's why it attacked us. Had we not resisted it, we too might have become mindless zombies - mere eyes and ears for Krob, searching, watching, exploring for him.'

She suddenly broke off, noticing how pale and shaken Derin appeared.

'Something is troubling you, boy,' she said. 'What is it?'

'You ... you say we might have become his eyes and ears,' he said falteringly. 'Does that mean the bowmen are ... are like extensions of Krob? Does he see through their eyes?'

'Yes, that's exactly what happens.'

Derin passed a hand distractedly across his forehead. He was paler than ever and there was a fine dew of perspiration on his upper lip.

'Then the situation is far worse than you think,' he said softly.

'Worse?' Asti broke in, puzzled. 'How can that be?'

Derin continued to stare directly at Marna.

'Tell me one thing,' he said, his voice hardly more than a whisper, 'is there anything which can stand against the power of the Staff?'

'Only the Sword of the old Kingdom,' Marna replied. 'Staff and Sword are equally matched in power, neither stronger nor weaker than each other.'

'In that case,' he declared, 'there is nothing that can save the land from destruction, because Krob now knows the whereabouts of the Sword.'

'How can that be?' Marna challenged him.

'This morning,' he explained, 'before the bowman died, he looked into my eyes and saw the Sword hidden in the box. That means Krob himself must know where it is. He's probably instructed one of his bowmen to steal it already.'

Marna shifted uneasily on the bed, the dry rushes crackling beneath her.

'I suppose it's possible ...' she began hesitantly.

'Possible!' Derin cried excitedly. 'What room is there for doubt?'

'I've told you before,' Marna said in an anxious voice, 'I refuse to speak of things I'm not certain ...'

But again he cut her short.

'You're just making excuses,' he said accusingly. 'You know very well what we found in the attic. And now Krob shares that knowledge. In all likelihood the Sword will be on its way to him even now. Isn't that so?'

'Couldn't you perhaps be mistaken . . . ?' Asti began, her voice trailing away as it became clear that nobody was listening.

'Come, be honest with me,' Derin said to Marna, determined to force a positive response from her.

Again she moved uneasily on the bed, the firelight casting deep shadows on her face. When at last she answered, it was in a tone of bravado.

'Even if what you say is true, what does it matter to us? I've told you already, let them fight their wars; let them kill each other. It's no business of ours. Our sole concern is to find your father and return to the uplands, as far away as possible from the plains and the mountains.'

'But don't you realize that what's happened is partly my fault!' Derin cried, feeling more and more exasperated by her. 'I'm the one who has put the ultimate control of the plains into Krob's hands. Every single person who dies or suffers in the coming war will be on my conscience.'

Marna clicked her tongue in disagreement.

'And what about your father?' she retorted. 'Isn't he also on your conscience? Didn't you run off and leave him? Or doesn't that matter?'

'Of course it matters,' Derin replied. 'But I can't put it right by pretending that I'm not responsible for Krob's discovery of the Sword. One more wrong can't wipe out the errors of the past.'

Marna ran her fingers irritably through her bush of grey hair.

'All right,' she said, 'let's both agree to forget the past - your cowardice, the Sword, everything. There's nothing we can do about it any longer. Neither you nor I nor anyone else can hope to stop Krob. From this moment on, we'll do only what is sensible: and that means finding your father and returning to the uplands where the warring forces will be most thinly spread. I'm sure it's what your father himself would want.'

'How would you know what he wants?' Derin replied bitterly.

'Because he's not a fool like you!' Marna answered fiercely, also rising to her feet.

Quickly, Asti jumped up to calm them.

'We can gain nothing by arguing amongst ourselves,' she said placatingly. 'Though at least one thing that Marna says is true: nobody can stop Krob. All any of us can hope to do is survive.'

But at this, Derin lost all patience.

'What about those who don't survive?' he said hotly. 'Don't other people matter? Is everything all right as long as we save our own skins?'

In his frustration, not fully aware of what he was doing, he raised the crutch and slammed the metal tip angrily onto the ground at his feet, leaving in the dust the now familiar imprint of the star and circle. It was exactly the same action he had performed earlier in the day, when he had been threatened by the black vapour. And now, as then, it had a marked effect: for Asti stepped hurriedly away, a look of surprise on her face.

'I ... I'm sorry,' she stammered out. 'I ask your forgiveness.'

Taken aback by Asti's sudden change of attitude, he glanced inquiringly at Marna; but the old woman seemed not to have noticed anything unusual.

'What is it?' Derin asked.

'I didn't realize ...' Asti replied with downcast eyes. 'I had no idea ... it was so hidden ...'

'What are you talking about?' he said, and again turned to Marna.

But they were interrupted by a hoarse cry from outside:

'Craak! Craak!'

'It is the raven!' Asti said in an awed voice. 'He has returned.'

'Haven't you any eyes in your head?' Marna said sharply. 'Didn't you see him perched on the headstone before you entered the cave?'

'It was dark,' she replied, 'I didn't ...' She paused as another thought came to her: 'How did he know you were here?'

'We brought him with us,' Derin explained.

'Ah,' she cried softly, a light of understanding touching her features.

She made as if to move towards the doorway; but Marna placed a detaining hand on her shoulder.

'That was a cry of warning,' she murmured.

They all three stood quite still, listening. From down the slope there came the clink of metal against rock. Then a harsh voice called out:

'Whoever you are in there, come out!'

'It's the soldiers!' Derin whispered. 'What can we do?'

'Nothing,' Marna answered resignedly, 'we're trapped.'

'No!' Asti said with sudden determination. 'They shan't find you!'

Taking Derin and Marna by the hand, she led them to the back of the cave, to the now empty alcove.

'Hide in here,' she said quietly. 'I promised Obin that I would bind my life to this rock. Now I will keep that promise.'

And she pushed them into the alcove and slid the rock back into place.

From within that dark, cool space, Derin and Marna listened as Asti called to the soldiers from the cave mouth. A minute or two later there was a tramp of heavy footsteps entering the cave.

'It's as I suspected,' the harsh voice rasped out, 'she's a witch! Take her! The rest of you, search the cave.'

Asti's voice rang out sharply in reply:

'There's no one here except me.'

Her tone carried such conviction and authority that the footsteps which had begun to advance deeper into the cave faltered and stopped.

'She's right,' someone said, 'the cave's empty.'

'Then why are there three bowls on the floor?' the harsh voice asked.

'Don't you understand anything?' Asti answered scornfully. 'I've been feasting with the wandering spirits of the Grove. They disappeared into the air as soon as they heard your men blundering around out there. But never fear, they are watching you even now.'

There was an immediate murmur of protest from the assembled soldiers. Someone said anxiously:

'This is a bad place. Let's get away from here.'

'You would be advised to leave me behind,' Asti said threateningly. 'Otherwise the spirits of the Grove will pursue you through the darkness.'

'Be silent!' the harsh voice ordered. 'We care nothing for your threats. You will come with us - at least one witch will ascend the gallows when we reach Iri-Nan.'

Derin and Marna, standing close together within the darkened alcove, listened to the footsteps leaving the cave. When all was still, Marna mumbled to herself for several moments and then, after tapping the heavy stone slab lightly with her fingertips, slid it easily aside.

The fire was still burning and all was exactly as they had left it - except that now Asti was no longer in the cave.

'That was too close for comfort,' Marna said, mopping her forehead.

'Is that all you can say?' Derin asked, amazed at her callousness.

'What else is there to say?' Marna answered, yawning and stretching as she hobbled wearily towards the bed.

'For goodness' sake!' Derin said in an irate whisper. 'She's just saved our lives! Doesn't that mean anything to you?'

'It means she's captive while we're still free,' Marna said deliberately. 'And that's all I know, so don't start asking me about why she acted as she did, because I have no more idea than you have.'

Derin half turned away in disgust.

'Aren't you even puzzled by her motive?' he asked. 'Hasn't it occurred to you that her action doesn't altogether make sense. Think back - half an hour ago she was agreeing with you, saying the only thing we can do is save our own skins. Then she turns round and does the very opposite.'

'Well, I suppose that's our good fortune,' Marna replied shortly.

With a weary sigh, she stretched herself out on the reed bed and closed her eyes. But at the sight of her lying there so peacefully, all Derin's former frustrated anger flared out once again

'You're lying to me!' he said accusingly, 'the way you have all along. You pretend that you understand so little, but you always know far more than you're prepared to tell me. Well, I'm sick of all your lies and your talk of trust - I want the truth for once!'

Marna opened one eye and looked at him standing there red-faced and angry in the firelight.

'There are times,' she said calmly, 'when lies are the shortest, surest road to the truth. You could almost say that sometimes lies are the only such road – at least the only road left open to us.'

And giving him just the suggestion of a smile, she rolled over onto her side and fell into a peaceful sleep.

8. The Woodlands

Derin awoke before dawn. Marna had already risen and relit the fire over which she was heating the remains of the stew. He watched her through half-closed eyes, noticing how old and tattered she appeared: her cloak torn and patched; her face, framed by its unruly mass of grey hair, both wrinkled and careworn, and also oddly determined – the prominent nose and chin thrust aggressively forward in the dancing firelight. As though sensing that she was being observed, she peered across at him.

'Time to get up, child,' she said, her voice unusually gentle, as if she had been caught unawares. 'We must be on our way by first light.'

He stretched and stood up, feeling sore and stiff from the hard ground and the days of travel. Already, through the open doorway, he could detect a faint greyness outside; and he quickly crouched before the fire and ate the stew that was given to him.

By the time he had finished, Marna had filled the inside pockets of her cloak with dried food and was ready to leave.

'Come,' she said impatiently, 'there's enough light to guide our feet.'

Putting down the bowl, he stood up slowly.

'One thing I want to be sure about before we set out,' he said. 'Where are we heading for?'

'Why do you ask such foolish questions?' she said irritably. 'You know we're making for the plains – for the city of Iri-Nan, where we're most likely to find your father.'

'What about Asti?' he asked. 'Aren't we going to try and find her too?'

'There you go again,' Marna said, shaking her head with disapproval. 'How many times must I tell you – we can't save the whole world. We're two small people who will be crushed like everyone else if we're not careful.'

'Asti isn't the whole world,' Derin said doggedly. 'She's someone who did us a great favour. She didn't have to help us, but she did.'

'She made her own choice,' Marna replied fiercely. 'Remember, we didn't ask her for her help.'

'And so do we just abandon her?'

'It isn't a question of abandoning her,' Marna said. 'It's just that we can't do everything, and our first duty is to your father. We have to find him. At all costs!'

There was a new note of urgency in her voice which puzzled Derin.

'Why are you prepared to sacrifice everyone for Ardelan's sake?' he said quietly. 'Asti is of the Witch People. Surely she's important too.'

'I've already told you,' Marna said, 'I owe Ardelan much. He's been good to me for many years. And come what may, I'll repay that debt.'

'We also owe Asti a debt,' he objected. 'After all ...'

He faltered, taken aback, as Marna flew into a passionate rage.

'What do you know of gratitude?' she screeched at him. 'It's bad enough that you've never loved Ardelan as you should. Now you want to make matters worse by deserting him. What's the matter with you, child? Can't you even feel affection for your own father? Are you becoming like Krob, who loves nobody but himself?'

Derin didn't reply for a moment. He had to admit that part of what Marna said was true. Try as he might, he could not feel any deep affection for Ardelan. For one thing, he could hardly remember him. His only vivid recollection had occurred in a dream, when Ardelan had silently appealed to him for help. And although he had been stirred by that appeal, he was moved to answer it more out of a sense of duty than anything else. Not for the first time, he now felt troubled by this strange lack of feeling on his part.

'I can't help being the person I am,' he said, staring thoughtfully into the dying flames of the fire. 'But I give you my word, I have no intention of deserting Ardelan. All I'm saying is that we should help Asti as well. It wouldn't be right just to leave her to die.'

Marna, her anger vanishing as suddenly as it had appeared, shuffled her feet uncomfortably, as though confused or embarrassed.

'All right,' she said at last, 'we'll do our best for her, but only on the condition that it doesn't endanger Ardelan's safety.'

Derin nodded his agreement and together they left the cave.

Outside, dawn had already broken. Beneath the grey sky of early morning the forest looked dark and mysterious, draped in a thin mantle of mist. Yet as on the previous day it held no fears for Derin: for him it was like a familiar place of refuge and he strode down the slope towards the tall, motionless trees. He paused only briefly, in order to look back at Craak who was still perched on the headstone. Raising one hand, he waved sadly, under the impression that the bird had at last come home, where it belonged, and would now remain near the cave – but Craak immediately launched himself from the headstone, alighting on Derin's shoulder with a cry of greeting.

'He's coming with us!' Derin said, happy yet surprised.

'There's cold comfort to be had from a grave,' Marna replied. 'The bird knows that. It's something we too might bear in mind.'

And with that grim warning, she strode off through the trees.

They hardly spoke in the hours that followed, walking one behind the other along the narrow trails. For Derin, journeying through the woodlands was a peculiarly pleasant experience and as he hurried after Marna he hummed to himself snatches of half-remembered songs.

The southerly direction they were taking led them steadily down towards the level of the plains; and with the passing hours the atmosphere became noticeably warmer, the trees and bushes more thickly covered with lush spring growth. By mid afternoon the woodlands had become a dense mass of green. All about them there was a profusion of life. Spring flowers pushed up through the soft leaf-mould; young branches, laden with heavy clusters of leaves, curved above their heads; deer and other small forest animals leaped away through the undergrowth. The only creatures not present were other human beings. Mile after mile passed and not a single person crossed their path. Occasionally they saw small bark huts, but they were always deserted. The whole of the woodlands, it seemed, was empty of people.

Yet that was not quite true. Towards evening they came to a clearing at the edge of which was a cluster of dwellings. Some were obviously inhabited because a haze of wood-smoke rose from the chimneys. Derin was all for avoiding them; but Marna dismissed his fears with a wave of the hand.

'Do you think the people here aren't aware of our arrival?' she said. 'There's nothing moves along the trails that they don't know of.'

As if to prove her point, she stood quite still in the gathering dusk; and soon there was a rustle of leaves above their heads and a small, dark-eyed man swung down to the ground. He bowed solemnly to them both, though never once taking his eyes from Derin and Craak.

'You are welcome,' he said, and led them towards one of the houses.

Inside, a large fire was burning in an open hearth. Two stools were placed before the hearth, as though in readiness for them; and on a low table were set bowls of steaming broth and a dish of hot potatoes. After indicating that they should sit and eat, the man left them, returning a few minutes later with the rest of the small community.

Nobody spoke until Derin and Marna had finished their meal. Then the man stepped forward and bowed once again, this time only to Derin.

'Master ...' he began.

But he got no further, for Marna let out a cackle of laughter.

'Oh, glory,' she said, wiping the tears from her eyes, 'this is no master. He's a mere boy, not even one of the Witch People.'

'But he carries the bird,' the man said gently.

'Aye, that's so,' Marna said, growing instantly serious. 'The bird's real master - Obin, whom you all knew - is dead; and the new master of the cave hasn't yet arrived. Even a bird can't mourn for long over a cold grave. He travels with us because the boy has a way with animals.'

There was a murmur of disappointment from the onlookers, but Marna ignored their response.

'Tell me,' she said, peering from face to face, 'what has happened to all your young men and women?'

The moment she spoke, Derin noticed for the first time that all the people around them were either middle-aged or old, as in the village of Solwyck. It was the man in whose house they were sitting who answered her, a ring of pride in his voice:

'They have gone to the mountains, like all the other young men and women of the woodlands.'

'With what purpose?' Marna asked.

'To protect the Circle of elders and the precincts of the Grove.'

Instead of replying, Marna turned and spat deliberately into the fire as a sign of disgust.

'But it is your own people that they wish to help,' the man protested, 'the elders of the Circle who are under attack from the...'

His voice died away as Marna again spat into the fire.

'Has anybody here heard of a young man called Krob?' she asked.

An old woman with red cheeks and thin white hair shuffled forward.

'I have heard of him, mistress,' she said meekly. 'He comes from Oak Tree Vale, a half-day's journey from here.'

'Tell us what you know about him,' Marna prompted her.

The old woman clasped her hands nervously.

'He was an orphan,' she said quietly, 'a poor wee thing who grew up without folk to care for him. A strange child who loved no one; who never cried or laughed as other children do. Even when an old childless couple took him in, it made no difference. Cold and withdrawn he was as a child; and cold and hard he grew into a man.'

Marna glanced fleetingly at Derin. He knew what that look meant: the coldness the old woman referred to was what Marna accused him of.

'Yes,' Marna said, 'that is a good description of Krob.'

And suddenly it seemed to Derin that she was speaking of this unknown thief as though she had known him, or at least known of him, for a long time - and once again Derin's smouldering doubts flared into life.

Unaware of what was going through Derin's mind, Marna went on:

'He is a creature who has lost the ability to feel emotion. Love, pity, sympathy - these are feelings that lie buried so deeply within him that he has forgotten what they mean. And it is this creature,

Krob, who now rules the Grove. It is to his aid that your young people have gone.'

'But why do you tell us this?' the man asked, obviously alarmed.

'Because if we fail . . .' she began, and quickly corrected herself, '. . . because if nobody succeeds in stopping Krob, war will sweep the land. Therefore let me give you due warning: if those times come, don't let anybody, not the soldiers nor the bowmen, tempt you to venture beyond the woodlands. Remain hidden here; go about your daily lives as you have always done; and tell other woodlanders you meet to do the same. For in that way you will be a tiny outpost of sanity in a world gone mad.'

'What of our children and grandchildren?' the old woman asked.

'You will serve them best by remaining free of the conflict,' Marna said sternly. 'If they ever return, they will need shelter and food, and you will be able to give it to them.'

Having delivered her warning, she stood up abruptly, ready to leave.

'But, mistress,' the man said, 'won't you sleep here in my house?'

Marna shook her head.

'No,' she said regretfully, 'even woodland folk cannot watch the paths after dark. If the soldiers came, you would be blamed for harbouring us.'

Derin followed her to the door; and after thanking their host for the food and warmth they stepped out into the darkened forest.

It was pitch black under the leafy boughs, with only a glimmer of star- or moonlight showing through gaps between the trees. Most of the time their only guide was the smooth feel of the path beneath their feet; and again and again they stumbled into trees or bushes. Once, after they had been travelling for over an hour, Marna fell into a patch of nettles. Only then, grumbling and swearing, did she agree to stop for the night.

Her intention was to lie down exactly where they were; but Derin took out his dagger and began digging a shallow hole in the soft earth.

'I'm glad you've found some use for that old thing,' she said, still in a grumbling tone. 'I'm surprised you haven't thrown it away.'

Derin paused for a moment, weighing the weapon in his hand.

He knew well enough why he kept it: not because of its usefulness, but rather because it was the only object he had rescued from the burned-out farmhouse. In that sense, it was like a known link with the past – a past which was otherwise shrouded in forgetfulness; and for that very reason he was unwilling to part with the dagger. Its simple, known shape and the solid feel of it in his hand reassured him; it was something, no matter how small and insignificant, which he could set against the mystery and threat which seemed to hem him in ever more tightly.

Grasping the hilt with both hands, he continued to dig until he had made a large shallow depression. Then he cut some supple young branches and arranged them in the depression to form a springy couch. He and Marna lay down on this, keeping close together for warmth – Marna chuckling to herself as she drew her cloak over both of them.

'Trust you to worry about your creature comforts,' she said.

But she was thankful enough for a soft bed and was soon fast asleep.

Although Derin was also tired, he lay awake thinking over the events of the day. One thing in particular stuck in his mind, something Marna had said to the woodland people that evening. Her exact words came back to him: 'Because if we fail . . .' She had corrected herself, but still the words had been spoken. What had she meant? What might they fail to do? She couldn't have been referring to Ardelan's rescue, because that could have no effect on Krob's power. Could it be, then, that she had another scheme in mind? Was the search for Ardelan merely an excuse? No, whatever else she intended, finding Ardelan was undoubtedly important to her; about that point at least, Derin was reasonably sure she wasn't lying.

What he was less sure about was her talk of returning to the uplands. That evening, when she had issued her warning to the woodlanders, she had spoken like someone who had no thought or hope of returning anywhere. Moreover, she had left immediately afterwards, as though her sole reason for visiting the cottages had been to issue that warning. And all that from a person who claimed to care little for others; who argued that with the days of the old Kingdom almost upon them, all she could do was try to survive.

Derin shook his head in bewilderment and snuggled deeper into the soft leaves and branches. Marna continued to breathe evenly and deeply beside him, and just before he fell asleep he asked himself whether perhaps he was being over-suspicious, creating mysteries where none existed.

That question was answered in the days that followed. On several occasions Marna stopped to visit small communities of woodlanders – just long enough to warn them to take no part in the coming trouble, to remain where they were, hidden and safe, far from the turmoil of war. Whenever she spoke in this way, Derin watched her face carefully, noticing how passionately she appealed to her listeners and with what respect they received her advice. It seemed to him that there was only one possible explanation for her behaviour, and on the fourth afternoon since leaving the cave he challenged her.

The forest had become more sparse around them, and taking advantage of the broadening pathway he drew alongside her.

'You come originally from the woodlands, don't you?' he said quietly.

She half turned her head, giving him a quick, searching glance.

'What makes you say that?' she said.

'Because you care about these people,' he replied. 'I've seen it in the way you speak to them, warning them of danger.'

He expected a denial from her, but she merely shrugged and laughed.

'In many ways you're still a child,' she said, 'lacking the guile of a man. Couldn't there be another reason for courting these people as I do?'

'What other reason?' he asked.

A sly look came into her eyes and she laughed again, more shrilly this time, an unpleasant sound that he flinched from.

'Think, Derin,' she said. 'It costs so little to be nice to them. And with luck we may come back this way. It's as well to know there are people near at hand ready to give us food and shelter.'

'Is it really your intention to return to the uplands?' he asked doubtfully.

But she never answered his question. She had already stopped and was pointing at something through the trees. He peered ahead and at first could see nothing but a dark line against the sky. It took him several seconds to realize he was gazing at the horizon.

'Have we reached the edge of the woodlands?' he asked excitedly.

Taking him by the hand, she led him to where the trees ended abruptly.

'The plains,' she said simply.

The ground sloped gently away from where they stood, and there, slightly below them, was the vast expanse of the great plain. Completely flat, interrupted by neither hill nor valley, it stretched away to the distant horizon. All that disturbed its even flatness was the occasional road or village. But even these were hardly noticeable at this time of year. On the plains the spring was already well advanced and the land was covered by a green sea of fresh young wheat, more brightly green than anything Derin had ever imagined.

'In the far distance,' Marna said, 'you can just see Iri-Nan.'

He followed the direction of her pointing finger and made out the dim shape of the city: a solid mass of stone buildings surrounded by cliff-like walls that rose straight up from the plain; and right in the centre, soaring high above everything else, a tall thin structure.

'Is that a tower in the middle?' he said.

'That,' she replied, her voice dropping to a whisper, 'is the Citadel. It was once the King's stronghold, where the Sword was kept.'

'And now?' he asked.

'They say it's where the Council meets.'

'But how are we ever going to get there?' he said. 'The land's as flat as a board; there's nothing to give us cover.'

'We can travel only one way,' she said. 'That's by road, and at night.'

There was no arguing with that decision, and for what remained of the day they lay in the sun or ate the dried provisions which Marna had brought from the cave. Derin was only too thankful for the rest. But Marna couldn't remain still for very long: she would doze for ten minutes, then start awake and walk impatiently to and fro, obviously frustrated by the delay, her eyes darting anxiously towards the east as though she expected some sign of Krob's growing power to appear at any moment.

When the sun finally set, she strode down the slope, leaving Derin to catch up as best he could. They reached a dusty road as the light was fading. In the gathering darkness they hurried on, the road leading them towards a cluster of lights that suggested the presence of a village. As they drew close, they could see that it was little more than a hamlet: twenty or thirty cottages grouped around a central meeting-hall and tavern. It was the very smallness of the place which persuaded them to follow the road straight through it rather than take temporarily to the fields.

Keeping close to the overhanging roofs of the cottages, they made their way cautiously forward. Nothing happened to alarm them until they had almost reached the open space between the hall and the tavern. Then they were alerted by the sound of strident voices. Peering around one of the cottages, they saw a group of helmeted soldiers standing outside the tavern laughing and talking. As they watched, the tavern door opened and another soldier, bareheaded and taller than the others, emerged.

'You men there!' he barked out. 'Come and fetch this food and water.'

It was the same harsh voice which had called to Derin and Marna when they had been hidden in the cave. As the men stepped forward, the light from the tavern window spilled onto his head and shoulders, revealing long pale features and blond hair; and with a start Derin realized he was the soldier who had confronted them at both Sone and Solwyck.

Meanwhile, the other soldiers were grumbling amongst themselves.

'It's dangerous going anywhere near a witch,' one of them said sullenly. 'I've heard tell that if you look into their eyes you're done for.'

Another added:

'Why not let her starve? She's going to die soon anyway.'

'Do as you're told and don't argue!' the pale-faced soldier replied coldly. 'She can't hurt you if you're in a group. As for the manner of her death, the Council will decide that. Our job is to get her to Iri-Nan.'

And thrusting a jug and plate into the hands of the nearest soldier, he turned and re-entered the tavern.

Derin, who had been watching all this, flattened himself against the wall of the cottage and whispered to Marna:

'They're talking about Asti. She must be here.'

Again he watched as the soldiers, still muttering resentfully, sauntered down the side of the tavern towards an old wooden barn at the rear.

'That's where she is,' he said excitedly, 'in that old barn.'

'And what do you intend to do about it?' Marna asked him.

'Do?' he said softly. 'Why, rescue her of course.'

But all at once Marna grasped him roughly by the shoulders.

'Listen to me,' she whispered, 'this is not the time for such a rescue. Even if you succeeded, you'd only warn them of our whereabouts; and then it would be doubly difficult to help Ardelan. Be patient, boy: let's find Ardelan first; after that we can try to get her free.'

'But she may not be alive by then,' Derin objected.

'That's the chance we'll have to take,' Marna said, a peculiar undertone of desperation creeping into her voice.

Derin drew back and tried to see her face in the shadows – the fiercely glinting eyes; the long nose curving aggressively over the sunken mouth.

'What makes you so ruthless?' he said calmly. 'Tell me that.'

'You know perfectly well,' she answered in a shrill whisper.

'No,' he said evenly, 'I know very little. I feel as though I'm caught up in a web of half-truths and lies. Why can I remember nothing of the past? What are you hiding from me? What is your real purpose?'

But she merely drew further into the shadows.

'You're imagining things,' she said in the same desperate tones. 'I'm hiding nothing from you. You have to trust me. You have to!'

Craak, sensing the tension between them, stirred uneasily on Derin's shoulder. With his free hand, he calmed the bird.

'So you can't give me a good reason why we should desert Asti?' he said.

'I've already given you reason enough,' she replied shortly.

'In that case,' he said quietly, 'there is only one thing to be done.'

He was about to turn away when Marna again grasped him firmly.

'If you endanger our quest by going to Asti now,' she hissed at him, 'then the trust is broken between us. And without trust, we can go no further together: we must part here, on this spot.'

There was no anger in her voice: only a desperate intensity. Derin hesitated, not because he doubted what should be done, but because he felt an unexpected pang of regret at the thought of parting with this strange old woman whom he distrusted, yet felt oddly drawn to. There was, he recognized, more than just a bond of trust to be broken – there were also bonds of friendship and of grudging affection. Gently, acting on the spur of the moment, he reached out and touched her withered cheek and lips.

'Go well, Marna,' he said softly.

She jerked her head away and turned her tear-filled eyes to the wall.

'Damn you, Derin!' she said in a choked whisper. 'Damn you! If only you realized ... if only ...'

But he could no longer hear her, for he was already scurrying towards the barn at the back of the tavern.

9. Captive

As Derin limped towards the barn, he could hear the soldiers talking inside. Quickly he hid behind the water butt that stood at the back corner of the tavern and watched as the soldiers emerged from the barn.

'If I had my way,' one of them said, 'I'd hang her here and now.'

'I agree,' someone else said. 'The time for questions and delays is over. We've got to show these bowmen and their kind what we're made of.'

They continued to mutter their threats and opinions as they made their way back to the front of the tavern. Not until they were past did Derin leave his hiding place. Standing in the darkened doorway, he called softly:

'Asti, where are you?'

'Derin! I'm here!'

Her voice, surprised and relieved, came from close at hand. As his eyes grew accustomed to the more intense darkness, he was just able to make out her shadowy form: she was sitting on a bale of straw only yards from the doorway.

'Come on!' he urged her. 'We have to get out of here quickly.'

'I can't,' she said, and held up both hands.

He saw then why she had been sitting there so meekly: her wrists were manacled and chained - the chain looped securely around a thick plank of wood that was nailed to two of the upright posts supporting the roof.

'Wait a minute,' he said.

He groped along the side walls until he found a shovel with a sturdy metal blade. Thrusting the blade between the plank and one of the upright posts, he took a firm grip on the handle and pulled. There was a sharp report, like the crack of a stock-whip, as the nails holding the plank gave slightly. Again he pulled and again there was a sharp crack. Already he could hear voices calling from outside, but it was too late to stop. He tugged frantically at the shovel, and with an extra loud creak the plank pulled away. Swiftly, Asti slipped the chain free and together they hurried to the open doorway.

But the soldiers, fully alerted, were already running down both sides of the tavern. A familiar voice called out:

'Stop exactly where you are!'

'This way,' Derin whispered, and led Asti to the corner of the barn.

To their relief, they found they were at the very edge of the hamlet: before them, hidden by the night, lay the great plain; and hand in hand they scurried towards the safety of this dark expanse.

But they had forgotten about the possibility of sentries, and before they had gone very far a soldier stepped out of the darkness ahead.

'Halt!' he cried, and jabbed his spear threateningly towards them.

Until then, Craak had clung tightly to Derin's shoulder. Now he took off and flew straight at the sentry, beating at his face with broad wings. The man ducked, jabbing at the bird with his spear. And in that instant Derin darted forward, the crutch whirling above his head. Before the sentry was even aware of this new danger, Derin had clipped him deftly across the side of the head, below the line of his helmet, and knocked him unconscious.

Yet that brief delay had given their pursuers time to catch up. There was a pounding of feet behind him and Derin turned to meet this new attack. As he did so, Craak let out a warning cry, something brushed past Derin's cheek, and the advancing soldier suddenly dropped his sword and clutched at the shaft of an arrow which had lodged in his throat. It all happened so quickly, leaving Derin so surprised, that he didn't even step aside. The stricken soldier staggered towards him, carried forward by his own impetus, and Derin caught him in his arms. Holding the man close against him, he noticed with astonishment how young he was: this face, only inches from his own, was the face almost of a boy - unlined, beardless, innocent - guiltless of these events in which he had been caught up.

'You're going to be all right,' Derin murmured reassuringly.

But the soldier's eyes had already rolled back and Derin found to his dismay that he was holding a dead weight.

Lowering the body gently to the ground, he turned and faced the darkness. There, standing knee-deep in the waving wheat, was a bowman. He was shorter than the bowman who had died near the woodlands, but otherwise identical: he wore the same long cloak, the same heavy muffler around the lower part of his face; and in his hands, bent and ready for release, was a short, powerful bow.

'No!' Derin shouted. 'Don't!'

For he could already hear other heavy footsteps behind him.

With a twang, the arrow was released, speeding past him - this time failing to find the soldier's throat, but slicing along the line of his jaw. With a cry of pain the man clutched at his face and fell forward.

Calmly, the bowman produced another arrow from the folds of his cloak and notched it onto the string, raising the bow once more in the direction of the pounding footsteps. But now Derin didn't hesitate.

'I said that's enough!' he shouted, and stepped directly into the line of the bowman's aim.

In the split second which followed, he seemed to see everything in slow motion: the bowman jerking the bow to one side in a futile attempt to deflect the arrow from its path; the arrow itself, like a single point of light in the surrounding darkness, speeding towards his throat; and his own deliberate movement as he thrust the crutch defensively before him. There was a brief delay, in which he waited motionless: then in sheer wonderment he watched as the arrow struck the stout shaft of the crutch and splintered into a dozen fragments.

Recovering quickly, Derin thumped the metal tip of the crutch down onto the dry soil.

'There must be no more killing!' he cried authoritatively.

He heard someone stop behind him; but he didn't turn around, taking care to keep himself between the soldier and this gloomy figure of death.

'Go back to where you come from,' he added, 'I have no need of you.'

Slowly and reluctantly the bowman slipped the bow back into

his cloak. That done, he raised a thin pale hand and pointed towards the tavern.

'Beware the Witch of Sone,' he said in his hollow, ghostly voice, 'she leads you to your death.'

And then, before Derin could reply, he vanished into the darkness.

'Wait!' Derin called out.

He was about to follow when someone caught him from behind and spun him around. He found himself staring at the tall pale-faced soldier whom he had first encountered in the inn at Sone.

'You!' the soldier said, his eyes narrowing at the sight of Derin.

Other soldiers had already run up and grabbed hold of Asti. One of them, a rough-looking fellow with a wispy blond beard, said angrily:

'You've had your way so far, Arith, and now one of our comrades is dead and another's wounded. I say let's string them up and be done with it.'

Arith, who was obviously the man holding Derin, drew his sword and faced the rest of his men.

'While I'm the leader,' he said warningly, 'there'll be no summary hangings. We've been instructed to take any Witch People before the Council, and that's what we'll do.'

'Even if it costs us our lives?'

'Even then,' Arith said calmly. 'Now take the girl back to the barn.'

As soon as his men had gone, Arith turned and looked at Derin.

'You saved my life a minute or two ago,' he said, eyeing his captive suspiciously. 'Why did you do it?'

'I'm sick of all the violence,' Derin answered truthfully. 'Someone has to try and stop it.'

'Were you sick of violence when you struck me down at Solwyck?' Arith asked, fingering the base of his throat.

'That was different,' Derin said. 'I was only defending myself then. It's the killing I object to – that has to stop.'

'You object to killing,' Arith said quickly, 'and yet twice now you've been defended by the bowmen. Can you explain why that should be so?'

Derin shrugged helplessly.

'It's one of the many things I don't understand,' he said.

'Come, boy,' Arith answered, 'don't take me for a fool. What is your connexion with the Grove?'

'I have no connexion with the Grove,' Derin said desperately. 'I've never seen these bowmen before. They suddenly appear; that's all I know.'

Arith stroked his chin thoughtfully.

'Very well,' he said at last, 'I expect you have your reasons for lying and I'm not one to force them out of you. My one duty is to take you to Iri-Nan, and with the men watching me I can't do otherwise. But given the chance, I'll do what I can for you. Not out of liking, mind: only because you saved my life. That's the greatest service anyone can do for me and I'll not forget it. Now let's get back to your witch friend.'

Taking Derin firmly by the arm, he was about to lead him away when he noticed the dagger at his side. Glancing around to make sure they weren't being observed, he murmured:

'That may be of some use to you later, but keep it out of sight. And remember, I'm trusting you not to use it on us.'

Derin pulled it free and slipped it inside his tunic. Then, together, they returned to the barn where Asti had already been chained up. Aware that it was useless to struggle, Derin stood quietly while manacles were locked onto his wrists and he too was chained to one of the posts.

'We set out at dawn,' Arith said, 'so you'd better get some rest.'

But just as he and his men were leaving the barn, there was a violent commotion outside and Marna, struggling and cursing, was dragged through the doorway by another group of soldiers.

'We found her near by,' they told Arith, 'skulking in the shadows.'

'Let me go,' she screamed, 'or I'll place a curse upon you all!'

Arith nodded to his men, indicating that they should release her. He immediately had cause to regret that decision: for the moment she was free she raised both hands and transfixed the man nearest to her. She was turning to another of the soldiers, her fingers spread menacingly, when Arith struck her hard across the face, sending her tumbling back amongst the bales of straw. She rose shakily to her feet, blood dribbling from her mouth, only to find herself staring at the point of Arith's sword.

'You can't bewitch us all, old woman,' he said steadily, 'and if you try, I'll cut off both your hands. Is that understood?'

Even Marna's anger cooled at such a threat.

'May the bread turn sour in your mouth,' she mumbled, 'and may the days of your life grow stark and cold.'

Yet in spite of her words she made no further attempt at resistance, her eyes glowing with suppressed resentment.

'I care nothing for your curses, witch,' Arith said. 'The chances are, you'll grow stark and cold long before I.' And then to his men: 'Chain her up like the others.'

She submitted to the fixing of the manacles, saying nothing until all the soldiers had left the barn.

'A fine pickle you've got us into,' she grumbled when they were alone.

'I thought you were going on without me,' Derin said.

'What chance did I have?' she replied, wiping the blood from her chin with a corner of her cloak. 'You two made enough fuss between you to wake the whole village. A mouse couldn't have crept away without being seen.'

For the first time since leaving the woodlands, Derin couldn't help smiling.

'Why don't you be honest and admit you had no intention of leaving me here?' he said. 'That was just an empty threat of yours. You were waiting around outside, weren't you? Watching for a chance to help us?'

'You think you're mightily important all of a sudden,' she retorted.

'Important enough to make you change your mind,' he said with a laugh.

'A lot of good it's done me,' she grumbled. 'Look at the mess we're in now.'

'At least we're sure of getting to your precious Iri-Nan,' he replied. 'Also, we're not quite as helpless as we might appear.'

And he produced the dagger from inside his tunic.

Marna leaned forward eagerly, saw what he was holding, and turned away in disgust.

'A fat lot of good that will do us,' she said.

'It's more useful than your witchery,' he said, poking fun at her.

And he laughed again, for despite the danger of their position, he couldn't help feeling oddly light-hearted. It needed only a moment's reflection for him to realize why that was so. Ever since leaving the upland farm, he had been wandering in a haze of confusion and doubt. Now he could at least understand what was happening to him - he was no longer stumbling in the dark. And although he was alarmed at the prospect of having to face the Council at Iri-Nan, he was at the same time reassured by it. It was a specific event whose meaning he could grasp; and to that extent it was preferable to following Marna wherever she cared to take him.

At the thought of Marna, he recalled the bowman's warning: 'Beware the Witch of Sone, she leads you to your death.' Was that really the truth, he wondered. He glanced across to where she sat leaning against the post, her face still dark with anger at the indignity she had been forced to suffer. Did she really intend him harm? It was impossible to tell - her moods changed so quickly. With a sigh of relief he realized that there was no need to worry about such things now. It didn't matter any more whether Marna intended him good or ill, for he was no longer in her hands. She, like him, stood at the mercy of the Council.

With that settled in his mind, he was about to make himself comfortable for the night when a familiar sound caught his attention and Craak sailed through the open doorway and landed lightly on his shoulder.

'Craak,' the bird croaked, its beady eyes gleaming in the darkness.

Asti, who had been silent until now, immediately sat up.

'All shall be well!' she burst out, a triumphant expression on her face. 'See! The bird still comes to you. What better proof ...'

Marna's voice cut sharply across what she was saying.

'Be quiet, girl! Cease your foolish chatter!'

'She has as much right to speak as you,' Derin said.

'That may be so,' Marna replied, 'but still there are things which should not be spoken before the ears of ignorance.'

'By ignorance, you mean me, don't you?' Derin said indignantly.

'I mean only that the Witch People should keep certain things to themselves,' Marna replied.

'But I thought . . .' Asti began.

'Never mind what you thought, girl!' Marna said, cutting her short once again. 'Rather you should remember what Obin taught you: that true knowledge follows the path of self-discovery.'

'And what is that supposed to mean?' Derin asked.

'Never you mind,' she said mysteriously, 'it's no concern of yours.'

Derin was too tired to argue any longer. With a sleepy yawn he settled himself in the straw; and within minutes he was fast asleep.

He was woken just before dawn by Craak's departure. He sat up and, through the doorway, saw a lantern bobbing towards the barn. A soldier entered and kicked at each of them in turn.

'Wake up!' he shouted. 'We leave before sunrise.'

And so began the two most miserable days of Derin's life.

After a breakfast of thin gruel, he, Marna, and Asti were ushered outside and chained to the back of a wagon in which the soldiers carried their supplies. When the column of troops moved out, they were forced to stumble along behind the wagon. From that position they couldn't see where they were going; they were almost jerked off their feet by the wagon's uneven motion; and they were half choked by the dust raised by the great iron-bound wheels. The dust was perhaps hardest to endure: it got into their eyes and nostrils; it caked in their hair and settled in a fine white layer on their skins; and it made their throats dry and sore.

By midday they were all hot and tired, and the skin on their wrists was red-raw from the rubbing of the manacles. Derin found it especially difficult to keep going, hampered as he was by his lame foot and the necessity of handling the crutch. Yet for all of them the worst was still to come. In the early afternoon they entered the first village of any size they had encountered so far. On either side of the road there were crowds of people who had left their houses and their work in the fields to watch the column go by. They were quiet to begin with; but at the sight of Witch People, they immediately started to shout abuse and throw things at the captives.

'Kill them!' they shrieked out.

'Show them what happens to enemies of the plains!'

'We'll teach them not to send their bowmen against us!'

A rotten cabbage struck Derin on the back and sent him staggering forward. Bad eggs, overripe fruit, and a shower of stones followed, and soon his clothing was covered in filth and his skin was grazed in several places. Most of the soldiers roared encouragement to the onlookers. Only Arith sensed the danger of the situation: silencing his men, he ordered them to form a protective circle around the captives. After that, although the crowd continued to shout abuse, they stopped throwing things for fear of hitting their own men.

From then on they encountered a similar reception in every village. Derin, humiliated and bespattered with refuse, tried to close his ears to the cries of 'murderer' and 'traitor' that greeted them from every side. With straight back and expressionless face he limped on, his eyes fixed on the sky a mile or two ahead, where Craak circled in the sunlight. In an attempt to escape from the misery of his position, he imagined himself in Craak's place – sailing high above the plain, looking down on the sparkling green wheatfields: the road reduced to a thin whitish line far beneath him; the villages like toy miniatures of real settlements. For a minute or two he could almost feel the wind cool upon his hot dusty face, his body buffeted gently by the currents of air. Then the cries of abuse broke through his reverie and he was back on the road, being jerked forward by the wagon, stumbling over the rutted surface.

Never had he been so relieved to see the sun sink below the horizon as he was that evening. They had reached an outlying farmhouse where Arith, worried by the attitude of the villagers, decided to stop for the night. The soldiers were housed in a big storage barn and the three captives were chained up in a small open shed near by. Derin, feeling totally disheartened by his ordeal, sank down on the straw and closed his eyes. Beside him he could hear his companions groaning with fatigue. None of them moved until bread and water were brought; then they sat up and ate and drank greedily, gnawing at the coarse bread as though it were sumptuous fare.

The meal revived them slightly and for a while they sat whispering together about the events of the day.

'Why does everybody hate us so?' Asti said, her young face pained by the memory of what had happened to her.

Marna plucked distractedly at the frayed edge of her cloak.

'They think we're to blame for the death of their men,' she replied.

'But why should they think that?'

'The Witch People have always been associated with the Grove,' Marna said, 'and by now the people know that they're being directly threatened by the Grove itself. You saw what the bowman did last night. Wouldn't you hate anybody you thought was associated with creatures like that?'

'Are there so many bowmen, then?' Derin asked.

'There are probably twenty or thirty,' Marna said, 'scattered throughout the plains and uplands. I'm only guessing, but I don't think even Krob's power could sustain more - not without hampering his other activities.'

'What other activities?' Derin asked.

'You saw how deserted the uplands were,' Marna answered, 'and how only older people are left in the woodlands. Krob's been recruiting as many men and women as he can. At this stage he must have a sizable army in the mountains. That's probably another reason why people here resent us so: they must have had news of that army, and judging by their reactions they're feeling threatened by it. For them, we're a visible embodiment of those forces, and so they hate and fear us at the same time.'

'Why don't they let us explain who we are?' Derin protested. 'It's not fair judging us like that without giving us a chance to speak.'

Marna laughed mirthlessly.

'Do you think that would help?' she responded. 'The face of fear has neither eyes nor ears. It is blind and deaf to all but its own terrors.'

They were interrupted by a movement somewhere in the darkness and a soldier appeared at the open side of the shed.

'Not so, witch,' he said. 'It's true enough that the plains folk hate you, but they have no fear in their hearts - not any more.'

'Have they all taken leave of their senses, then?' she replied sharply. 'Even a fool would have brains enough to fear Krob, crazed as he is by the power of the Staff.'

'No, there you're wrong,' the soldier contradicted her. 'The days of terror are past. Word has just arrived that the Sword of the Kings is being held in the Citadel. There's been gossip to that effect for some time; and I'll grant you that much of it was wishful thinking to begin with. But now it's really happened: the Sword has recently been found and there's power enough here on the plains to resist anything the Grove can bring against us.'

With a triumphant sneer he trudged off into the night once more.

'But what he says is impossible,' Derin broke out. 'We left the real Sword back there in the uplands.'

'Impossible or not,' Marna said gloomily, 'it bodes ill for the future. As long as the plains folk believe they have the Sword, they'll be prepared to go out against Krob – you heard the soldier, how confident he was. And once the real conflict begins, it'll be no easy matter stopping it.'

'In that case we have to get to Iri-Nan without delay,' Asti said urgently. 'Something has to be done.'

'We'll get there soon enough,' Marna said, 'though goodness knows what we can do. All I ever hoped for was to rescue Ardelan. It wasn't much to ask for, yet it seems even that will be denied us.'

They spoke no more that night, thankful to curl up in the straw and rest their aching bones. Before dropping off to sleep, Derin was disturbed briefly by the reappearance of Craak. The bird glided silently into the shed and gently stirred his hair with its beak, as though trying to comfort him. Derin stroked the smooth black feathers and again made himself comfortable, falling quickly asleep. Every hour or two after that he would half wake and turn over, reassured by the sight of the bird standing guard.

He came fully awake shortly before dawn and took the bird in his hands for what he knew might be the last time.

'You've been a faithful friend,' he whispered gratefully.

The bird opened its beak and softly uttered the only sound it knew:

'Craak.'

But to Derin's ears it said so much, speaking to him of love and trust and friendship – all those things he had looked for in Marna yet never really found: the wily old woman so much more complex and unpredictable than this simple creature. For several minutes the boy and the bird stared at each other: the soft human eye and the hard bright eye of the bird only inches apart. It was a period of strange peace, almost of happiness; then, reluctantly, Derin released Craak and watched as the bird flew away into the twilight.

That one brief period of stillness was the only real peace Derin experienced all day. The column was moving again soon after dawn, and with every mile covered, the vertical walls of Iri-Nan grew more huge and forbidding. There was a vastness about the city which dwarfed everything else. Like a gigantic mound of solid rock, it dominated the plain, unnerving Derin and making him wish he was back in the green glades of the woodlands. Yet in spite of this desire, his eyes were drawn again and again to those misty heights – to the enormous buttresses jutting out from the walls; to the great stones of the battlements, shimmering yellow-white in the sunshine, perched precariously above the even sheen of the wheat-fields; to the tower-like Citadel thrusting upwards until it threatened to pierce the blue dome of the sky.

As they drew closer to the city the road became more rutted, the villages more populous. People still lined the road as the column went by; but now, instead of shouting abuse and pelting the captives with refuse, they taunted and jeered at them. Derin, remembering what Marna had said on the previous evening, recognized in the jeering cries the perilous confidence she had referred to. At one point a young woman burst through the protective ring of soldiers and thrust her face close to his.

'We'll burn the Grove to a cinder!' she screamed. 'And you with it!'

The soldiers dragged her away, but the incident had an unsettling effect on Derin. He was disturbed not so much by the threat itself as by the hysteria in her voice and the insane gleam in her eyes. Her whole attitude created for him a far more vivid and terrifying impression of the war-crazed world of the old Kingdom than all Marna's dark warnings; so that, despite the heat of the day, he couldn't help shivering with apprehension. And when at last he reached the city gates he felt almost relieved, the solidity of the stone pillars and walls giving him a sense of assurance.

They entered the city through a broad stone archway. Passing beneath it, Derin thought nervously of the enormous weight poised above his head and immediately quickened his pace. But to his surprise, once he was inside the walls he found himself in a strangely closed and secure world. The streets were paved and narrow, hemmed in by tall stone buildings. Now, late in the afternoon, no sunshine reached the thoroughfares and the light was noticeably muted, like a kind of prolonged dusk. Wherever he looked, people were walking briskly past – most of them tall and fair-haired, typical of the plains region. Unlike the villagers, they paid the column little attention, too absorbed in their own activities. Occasionally someone would shout or shake his fist at the three chained figures, but the words or gestures were somehow swallowed up by the surrounding walls of stone and by the ceaseless bustle of city life.

The street they were in led directly to the heart of the city, a large open square that fronted the Citadel. At close quarters the Citadel was a soaring spire of stone pierced at regular intervals by narrow windows. As soon as they entered the square the column stopped, and Arith came over to the wagon and supervised the unshackling of his captives.

'You are now prisoners of the Citadel,' he said. 'In a few minutes the Captain of the Guard will appear and I will hand you over to him.'

While they waited, Arith drew Derin to one side.

'There is little I can do for you at the moment,' he murmured, taking care that no one should overhear them. 'Even so, I meant what I said back there: a man's life is dear to him and I shan't forget your saving me from the bowman. If I'm able to return the favour, I shall do so gladly.'

They were interrupted by the appearance of the Guard. A squad of twelve men, led by a magnificently dressed Captain, emerged from the doorway at the base of the Citadel and crossed the square. Derin moved closer to Asti and Marna and waited with downcast eyes. He heard the squad come to a halt and the even tread of the Captain's approach. A deep voice began:

'In the name of the Citadel . . .' and then it faltered and stopped.

Beside him, Derin was aware of Marna gasping with amazement. He glanced up, and immediately he too let out an exclamation of surprise. For standing before him, dressed in a resplendent scarlet cloak and holding the long bronze-headed spear of the Captain of the Guard, was his father, Ardelan.

10. Within the Citadel

In spite of Ardelan's magnificent appearance, Derin had no doubt about his identity. He was definitely the man in his dream - Derin would have recognized that high forehead and those deep-set eyes anywhere. Yet even now, with the familiar face before him, it failed to awaken any deeper memories of the past. Equally disturbing, it failed to stir in him any feelings of affection. He knew this man was his father; but as Marna had predicted, Derin could discover in himself none of the spontaneous love which it was normal for a son to feel.

He glanced sideways at Marna, to gauge her reaction. But as always her expression was difficult to read - her face showing an odd mixture of surprise and cunning.

'Is this some kind of trick ...?' she began.

Ardelan silenced her with a furtive movement of his hand.

'Hush!' he murmured. 'Do you want to get us all killed?'

In a louder voice, he said:

'I arrest you in the name of the Citadel. You are all three accused of being witches and of plotting against the Council.'

At a nod from him, the twelve-man guard stepped forward and marched the captives across the square. As they entered the Citadel, Derin caught a glimpse of a large hall before he was pushed towards a circular staircase and made to climb. There were no windows in the staircase, only flares, and the air was fetid and stale. Soon Marna, who was directly behind him, was gasping for breath; and he paused for a moment and looked back.

'She's an old woman,' he said. 'Why don't you let her rest?'

But the nearest soldier thumped him in the back and made him go on.

They continued to climb for some time, until they reached a landing with a heavy wooden door on one side. By then Marna's breath was coming in searing gasps, and she could barely stand. Two of the guards dragged her to the door, opened it, and threw her inside. Asti and Derin were pushed in after her, and the door closed and locked.

There was no time to inspect their surroundings. Marna had slumped forward onto her knees, her face deathly pale, her lips pinched and blue. Between them Asti and Derin carried her across to the far corner and laid her gently on a rough bed of straw.

'Do you think she'll be all right?' Asti asked in a worried voice.

'I don't know,' Derin said doubtfully.

To him the old woman appeared to be seriously ill. But he had underestimated her toughness, for within minutes she was breathing far more easily and some of the aggressive twinkle had come back into her eyes.

'They can't dispose of me as simply as that,' she said hoarsely. She started to chuckle, but fell prey to a fit of coughing.

Leaving her to recover, Derin took stock of their prison. They were in a triangular-shaped room lit by two narrow openings in one of the walls. The ceiling and all three walls were made of quarried stone, as was the floor which was strewn liberally with sand. Through one of the slit openings Derin could see a sliver of blue sky and he went and looked out. It came as no surprise to discover how high they were, far above the level of the battlements. Below him he could see the tops of the many buildings, the narrow streets winding through the city and, beyond the outer walls, the vast green expanse of the wheatlands.

He was still contemplating this scene when the door opened behind him and Ardelan entered alone. Marna immediately struggled to her feet.

'Well?' she said. 'What do you have to say for yourself?'

'There's time enough for explanations, old woman,' he said. 'First let me see my son.'

And he strode across the chamber and placed a hand on Derin's shoulder. Derin, ashamed of his lack of feeling, raised his head and looked into his father's face. Instantly he sensed something was wrong. The mouth was smiling at him, but the eyes were cold. No matter how deeply he gazed into them, he could discern no trace of love or warmth. They were the eyes almost of a stranger: not unkind, merely distant and reserved.

'You are welcome, my son,' Ardelan said.

And he kissed Derin first on the forehead and afterwards on each cheek, as was the custom in upland families.

'Is this how you show your welcome?' Marna asked, some of the shrill quality coming back into her voice.

'Take care, old woman,' he said with a smile, 'don't push my love too far. I'm all that stands between you and death in this place.'

'What worries me,' Marna answered fiercely, 'is how you come to hold such a position. A common soldier is one thing, but Captain of the Guard! Are you going to tell me you've willingly joined this rabble?'

'This is no time to talk of people as rabble,' Ardelan said severely. 'Haven't you heard what's happening in the east? We all need to stand by each other in such times as these.'

'Oh, I see,' Marna said sarcastically, 'and I suppose the plains folk were standing by us when they put us in chains.'

'You can't really blame them,' Ardelan replied. 'They have reason enough to be suspicious of all strangers - of Witch People especially.'

'Can't blame them!' Marna burst out angrily. 'What do you expect me to do, thank them for the past two days of misery? Has that piece of red cloth you're wearing robbed you of your senses? Why . . .'

But she was interrupted by Asti.

'It is foolish to dwell on such resentments,' she said gently.

Derin nodded his agreement.

'What's more,' he reminded Marna, 'we didn't come all this way to quarrel.' Then turning to his father: 'We expected to find you serving as a common soldier. How did you become Captain of the Guard in so short a time?'

'Ah, there I was lucky,' Ardelan said.

'You call it luck!' Marna broke in indignantly.

'Hear me out,' he pleaded. 'Under normal circumstances you wouldn't have found me in Iri-Nan. By now I would be serving on the eastern road. But something unusual happened upon my arrival here in the city.'

'What was that?' Asti prompted him.

Ardelan walked over to the narrow window-opening and looked down.

'We were assembled in the square,' he began. 'There were about a hundred of us, all new recruits, being handed over to the Guard, when suddenly a bowman appeared and shot the Captain of the Guard through the heart. Nobody expected it and everyone scattered, the guards included. I don't know why I didn't run with the rest - perhaps I was too scared to move. But all at once I found I was standing there on my own, watching the bowman fit another arrow into his bow. There was only one thing I could do. This spear' - he held it up for them to see - 'was lying beside the Captain's body and I picked it up and threw it as hard as I could. I was only just in time. The bow was already bent when the spear struck him.'

'And did you kill him?' Derin asked.

Ardelan nodded.

'That same day I was made the new Captain of the Guard,' he went on, 'as a reward for my action. I'm now responsible for the Council's safety.'

While he had been speaking, Marna's anger had slowly given way to intense interest. Now she shuffled forward, her eyes blazing.

'You say you killed the bowman?' she asked urgently.

'Yes.'

'What happened to the dark power inside him? Did you see it leave his body?'

'He didn't die instantly,' Ardelan said. 'He crawled across the square and into the Citadel. It was in this building that the power left him.'

'Yes,' Marna said impatiently, 'but what happened to it?'

'I'm not sure. I saw it issue from his mouth, and after that it disappeared into the shadows of the stairwell.'

'You mean it's still here in the Citadel?' Marna said incredulously.

'Who knows? It could be anywhere now.'

'Who knows?' Marna echoed him, almost shouting the words. 'I for one know that it's still here somewhere. Do you think that having penetrated the Citadel it would leave of its own accord? I tell you it will work its mischief before it ever departs.'

'What mischief can it possibly work?' Ardelan objected. 'The whole of the Citadel is heavily guarded.'

'Aye,' Marna replied, 'it's guarded against a physical enemy, but not against this spirit of evil. It's not something you can cut down with a sword. Its hiding place is the mind. Have you looked into your men's eyes to see if it lurks there?'

'My guards are all hand-picked,' Ardelan answered. 'They are the most trustworthy men available.'

Marna clicked her tongue with annoyance.

'You're as foolish as your son in many ways,' she said. 'It's just as well we've found you. We must leave this place before the evil shows itself.'

Ardelan shuffled his feet and gave an embarrassed cough.

'Well?' Marna said irritably. 'What are we waiting for? It will soon be dark and you hold the keys to the whole of the Citadel. We can be well on our way to the uplands long before anybody knows of our absence.'

Ardelan coughed again and looked at Derin, as though for support

'I can't leave here,' he murmured at last.

Marna, who had already begun moving towards the door, stopped in her tracks, an expression of disbelief on her face.

'What are you talking about?' she said. 'You owe these people nothing. They burned your farm and attacked your son; they brought you here under threat. What reason is there to give them your support? Unless, of course, they've turned your head with that piece of red rag you wear.'

Ardelan shook his head slowly.

'It isn't vanity which makes me stay,' he said. 'As you know, I was unwilling to leave my farm. You saw how I fought for my freedom. But in the course of the journey here I witnessed things which made me change my mind - recruits and soldiers alike shot down by the bowmen who lay in ambush. They didn't ask us whether or not we supported the Grove; they killed men where they stood, showing no mercy. It didn't take me long to realize that what the soldiers said was true: the power of the Grove must be opposed. If it isn't, nobody will be safe. We shall all end up like the bowmen - a race of living dead.'

He paused and Marna, in a spirit of mockery, brought her hands together in a slow handclap.

'A very pretty speech,' she said scornfully. 'They can carve it on your headstone when they bury you in this foreign soil.'

'I have no intention of dying,' he said evenly.

'Nor have I,' Marna retorted. 'But I swear to you by the wisdom of Obin that if we stay here we shall all die, every one of us. Don't you realize that the Circle no longer rules the Grove? That Krob now wields the Warden's Staff? The Council and all who serve it will be helpless before him.'

'I know of Krob's power,' Ardelan answered, 'but it is not true that we are helpless. We too have a source of strength: the ancient Sword of the Kings has just been rediscovered. It is here in the Citadel, in the safekeeping of Illam, one of the members of the Council.'

'Are you sure of this?' Marna asked doubtfully, looking at Derin.

'I have seen the Sword with my own eyes,' Ardelan said. 'Illam now wears it at his side.'

'But that is unlawful,' Asti broke in. 'No ordinary member of the Council may carry arms within the Citadel. Obin himself told me that.'

'That is normally the case,' Ardelan admitted, 'but these are not normal times.'

Derin, who had been listening in some bewilderment, now moved closer to his father.

'How can you be sure it is the Sword of the Kings?' he objected. 'What proof have you been given?'

'The proof of my own eyes,' Ardelan said. 'Never has there been a Sword to match it. When you see it you will know what I mean.'

'When we see it?' Marna took him up quickly. 'What are you saying, man? Are you going to abandon us to the judgement of the Council?'

Ardelan lowered his eyes, leaning heavily on the spear he carried.

'I have no choice,' he said in subdued tones. 'I am now a servant of the Council.'

Marna stepped towards him and placed one withered hand on his arm.

'Think about what you're saying, Ardelan,' she murmured. 'What is more important: your duty to the Council or your love for your own kind?'

Gently but firmly, Ardelan removed her hand from his arm.

'Do you think I'd allow any harm to befall my son?' he said.

He turned towards Derin as he spoke, appealing to him much as he had in the dream. And once again Derin searched his face for signs of real affection; but the same cool, distant quality persisted there.

'If your son is so dear to you,' Marna said, 'why not protect him from the Council? Give him his freedom, while there's still time.'

'Yes, free him,' Asti added, speaking with peculiar urgency.

'No, that I cannot do,' Ardelan said sadly. 'I have sworn enmity to the Grove and allegiance to the people of the plain. I cannot go back on that oath. All I can promise you is this: that if the judgement of the Council is against you, I will put within your reach the possibility of escape.'

All Marna's gentleness dissolved instantly.

'Is that the best you can offer us?' she screamed at him. 'Your son risks his life to find you, and this is how you repay him!'

Her face flushed with indignation, she turned her back on Ardelan. But he remained unmoved by her anger.

'You will be taken before the Council tomorrow morning,' he said quietly, 'all three of you.' For the first time he looked directly at Asti: 'Are you also one of the Witch People?' he asked.

She nodded.

'I've studied their ways for eight years now,' she said.

'That is not something to boast of here in Iri-Nan,' he cautioned her.

'I do not boast,' she said quietly. 'I merely tell you the truth.'

'That may be so,' Ardelan conceded, 'but take my advice, both you and Marna: if you are challenged by the Council, deny any knowledge of the Witch People.'

'Are you asking us to lie at our own trial?' Asti asked him.

Ardelan walked over to the door where he paused, his hand on the latch.

'There are times,' he said deliberately, 'when lies are the shortest, surest road to the truth.'

Although they were not addressed to him, Derin recognized the words immediately: they were identical to what Marna had said to him in the cave, soon after Asti's capture. But before he could speak, Ardelan left, locking the door firmly behind him.

'Isn't that what I mentioned to you once?' Marna said, apparently unperturbed by this repetition of her own words. 'Believe me, it's good advice.'

'It may be what you believe,' Derin said uneasily, 'but that doesn't necessarily make it good.'

Marna merely chuckled to herself.

'Good or bad,' she said, 'what does it matter? Just as long as everything works out well in the end, the three of us safely out of here, and you and I on our way back to the uplands together.'

'No,' Derin answered deliberately, for here was something he had thought hard about during the past two days, 'we won't be travelling together to the uplands. If we're lucky enough to leave this place alive, I shall choose my own road. I'll follow at your heels no longer.'

Marna responded with a casual shrug.

'We can decide such things later,' she said easily. 'For the present, all I want is to rest my weary bones.'

And she lowered herself slowly onto the straw bed.

The shadows had already begun to gather in the chamber, and now they rapidly deepened into night. Before it became completely dark, the door was opened and a group of armed guards brought in food and drink and a small oil-lamp. The captives ate the simple meal in silence and afterwards lay down to sleep - Marna and Asti on the bed, Derin curled up in the corner. Once, in the course of the night, he was woken by a whirr of wings and he sat up hoping to see Craak appear in one of the narrow window-openings. But it was only an owl on its way to hunt for mice in the wheatfields.

Soon after dawn the same guards reappeared, this time not only with food, but also with three basins of water.

'The Captain has given orders that you should wash yourselves before going in front of the Council,' one of the soldiers said.

Gratefully, because they were still covered with heavy, cloying dust from the road, they scrubbed themselves clean and straightened out their crumpled clothing. Then, having eaten a meagre breakfast, they were taken down to the large hall on the ground floor of the Citadel.

Like their cell, it had a stone floor strewn with sand, but in every other respect it was far more splendid. Great chandeliers hung from the ceiling and the walls were covered with coloured hangings. In the middle of the floor a group of nine richly upholstered chairs had been arranged in a semi-circle; and behind the chairs, on the far wall, painted in red and gold, was the ancient sign of the Citadel: a sword enclosed by a circle of ten stars.

The sight of that pattern took Derin back to the day he had spent hidden in the attic; and beyond that to the afternoon he had woken in the wood and seen the same emblem printed in the soft snow. He was still contemplating that afternoon, which stood like an impassable barrier in the passage of his memory, when Ardelan entered with the rest of the guards.

'The Council is about to appear,' Ardelan warned them quietly.

To their right, one of the hangings was pulled aside and nine elderly men and women, all dressed in bright red robes, filed in and sat in the empty chairs. One of them in particular caught Derin's attention: the man Ardelan had referred to as Illam. He was a tall gaunt figure who walked with lowered head, his eyes fixed on the ground at his feet. Strapped to his waist was the most magnificent sword Derin had ever seen: the hilt was of gold and encrusted with gems; the scabbard, of gold and silver, bearing a circle of ten brilliant diamonds within which there glowed the ruby outline of a sword. Except for Illam, all the Councillors appeared slightly uneasy, as if they were troubled and also cowed by the presence of the ancient weapon.

It was Illam who now addressed the gathering, though still without raising his head, his eyes hidden by shaggy eyebrows.

'There is no doubt about the identity of the women,' he said, his voice strangely hollow in the high-ceilinged hall. 'Their dress alone betrays them. My only question is to the boy. Are you also of their tribe?'

Derin limped a few paces forward.

'I am not one of the Witch People,' he said. 'I am the son of an upland farmer and I've come here searching for my father.'

'Can you prove to me that this is so?' Illam asked solemnly.

Someone behind Derin called out:

'I can vouch for the boy.'

Everyone turned towards the sound of this unknown voice. Standing in the doorway of the hall was the tall, pale-faced figure of Arith.

'It was I who captured him,' he went on. 'He has none of the powers of the old woman. Moreover, on the night of his capture he saved me from a bowman. No witch would have done such a thing.'

'What do you know of witches?' Asti suddenly burst out. 'We too are the enemies of Krob.'

'Hold your tongue, girl,' Marna said, but she spoke softly, without any trace of harshness in her voice.

There was a brief pause, everybody waiting for Illam's response.

'Very well,' he said slowly, 'we accept the soldier's word. Therefore our judgement is this: that the boy goes free; and that the witch women be put to death.'

'But what have we done?' Asti said desperately.

'You have heard our verdict,' Illam said severely.

He had already risen to his feet and was about to leave. Derin, who had listened to the judgement with a mixture of joy and dismay, was almost tempted to remain silent. But one glance at Asti convinced him otherwise.

'Wait!' he called out loudly. 'You've given us only your verdict. What about the other members of the Council? What do they say?'

'I now speak for all the Council,' Illam answered angrily. 'Can't you see that I wear the Sword of the Kings?'

He made an impatient gesture with his hand and the other members of the Council also rose and began to file out - though not without exchanging worried glances amongst themselves. Their obvious uneasiness merely served to strengthen Derin's resolve, and raising his voice almost to a shout, he cried:

'You wear a fine sword, true enough, but it isn't what you claim it is.'

Immediately there was an unnatural silence as the Council members stopped and stared in Derin's direction, many of them clearly relieved to hear Illam challenged in this way.

'Take care, boy,' Illam said threateningly, 'or I might regret the mercy I've shown you.'

'Is the judge immune from judgement?' Derin answered quickly. 'What proof do you have that what you wear is truly the Sword of ancient times?'

Again there was a shocked, yet oddly approving silence.

'As most people know already,' Illam said in low menacing tones, 'this is no ordinary weapon. I learned of its whereabouts in a dream. In that dream I was told to go to a secret cave in the woodlands where a wise man called Obin would give me something with which we could defend ourselves against the power of the Grove. I undertook that journey some time ago, and this is what I was given - with the instruction that I should reveal it when the time was ripe. I tell you it is nothing less than the Sword of the Kings.'

Illam had hardly finished speaking when Asti shouted:

'That's a lie! Obin would never have given you such a thing!'

There was a gasp of amazement from everybody present and Illam quickly turned to face her, though still with his head lowered.

'You will pay dearly for that accusation,' he said.

He raised his hand to summon one of the guards; but before he could complete the gesture there was a beating of wings from somewhere high up near the ceiling and Craak came swooping down, the tips of his flight-feathers passing within inches of Illam's face. Startled, he raised his head for the very first time. And straight away Derin saw why he had kept his eyes hidden: they were flat and lifeless, the eyes of death itself.

Behind him, he heard Marna whisper:

'Beware, child, you are facing the spirit of the dead bowman.'

Derin knew from previous experience that where the bowmen were concerned it wasn't his own safety he had to consider. That deathly gaze was fixed not on him, but on Asti. Already Illam had drawn his sword and was stalking towards her. Now that he had been revealed he made no attempt to mask his true identity.

'She is mine,' he croaked out in a hollow whisper.

Asti seemed powerless to move: held by those dead eyes, she stood helpless before the advancing sword.

'Stop him!' Derin shouted.

And when the guards, shocked and confused, failed to intervene, he slipped the crutch from beneath his arm and stepped quickly to Asti's side.

'Keep back, boy,' Illam warned him in the same ghostly whisper, 'I have no quarrel with you.'

Something flickered and moved within those sightless eyes and for a moment Derin relaxed his vigilance. It was all that Illam needed. With astonishing speed he brought the sword crashing down. It was too late to pull Asti clear. As a pure reflex action, Derin thrust the crutch into the path of the descending blade. Even as he did so, he expected the bright steel to slice through the smooth wooden shaft. But the sharpened edge, instead of hitting the wood, caught the metal tip. There was a spray of sparks and a clang of shattered metal as the shock of the blow vibrated through Derin's arms; and the next thing he knew, Illam was standing before him with only the hilt of the sword in his hand, the blade having shivered into fragments. Casting the gem-encrusted hilt aside, Illam lunged for the crutch, his pale fingers closing on the wooden shaft. But before he could tighten his grip, Ardelan's spear flashed across the hall and pierced him through the chest, sending him crashing into the empty chairs. As he fell, the spear jutting from his chest, he let out a peculiar hissing sigh.

'Look out!' Marna cried loudly.

Derin grabbed the still helpless Asti and dragged her over to the wall. All around them people were crying out or ducking for cover. Only Illam remained completely still, his emaciated body stretched out on the stone floor, while from his mouth and nostrils there rose a dense black vapour. It hovered menacingly in the centre of the hall, as though carefully selecting its next victim. But Craak, who had been watching from one of the chandeliers, swooped once again. Almost at the same instant Marna darted forward, her fingers splayed. And the vapour, attacked from two directions, swirled in upon itself, and then, like a pall of smoke caught by the wind, shot away over the heads of the guards, out of the hall, and through the doorway of the Citadel.

'Quickly!' Ardelan shouted. 'Lock the doors!'

Guards pushed the heavy doors closed and secured them with

bolts and bar. When they returned to the hall, the remaining members of the Council had recovered from their shock and were huddled together whispering excitedly. One old woman signalled for Ardelan to approach.

'There is much to discuss,' she said, 'but one thing is clear: you have again done well. The Council will thank you formally when we next convene. Meanwhile, keep the prisoners safely. We will decide their fate later.'

Ardelan bowed obediently before her.

'It shall be done,' he said.

And having retrieved his spear from Illam's body, he led the three captives back up the staircase to their cell. Once inside, with the door closed, he turned and faced them.

'What happened down there?' he asked.

'It is as I foretold,' Marna replied. 'The spirit of the dead bowman was hiding here all the time – in the body of Illam.'

'And the sword?' Asti broke in, her face still pale from her recent ordeal.

'Ah, that was one of Krob's tricks,' Marna said. 'It was merely a bright toy planted here to mislead the Council, not the true Sword at all.'

'But why should he play such a trick?' Asti insisted.

'It is likely that Krob also seeks the true Sword,' Marna explained, 'and therefore he wanted the Council to believe the Sword was in their possession; that way, he could be sure they wouldn't impede his search. In addition, he knows that if the people of the plain are filled with false confidence – the kind of confidence the counterfeit sword has given them – they will more rapidly fall prey to the power he is mustering.'

Ardelan nodded thoughtfully.

'We must talk of these things further,' he said, 'but not now. If I remain too long with you, someone may begin to suspect my allegiance. For the moment you should be secure enough here – at least until the Council elects a new member to replace Illam. After that I can't answer for your safety. They must be seriously disturbed by what has happened today; and also ashamed of how easily they've been tricked into submission. For both of these reasons it is possible they might decide that the wisest and safest thing to do is to dispose of you – and that could include you, Derin, because Illam's judgement means nothing now.'

'Then let me remind you of your promise,' Marna said. 'You spoke yesterday of helping us to escape.'

'Don't worry, old woman,' he assured her, 'I'll honour that promise. Just give me time to think. I must somehow make it appear that you escaped without help from anyone in the Citadel.'

'That's easily accomplished,' Marna said with a sly smile. 'Tonight, after dark, send only two guards up with our food; and see that the outer door is left untended. Is that possible?'

'Yes, it can be done. Is there anything else?'

'No,' Marna said, still grinning slyly, 'leave the rest to us.'

'In that case,' he replied, 'I must now return to the Council.'

As on their first meeting, he kissed Derin on the forehead and cheeks.

'My only wish for you,' he murmured, 'is that you get far away from here. Go anywhere you think is safe. We'll meet again when this trouble is over.'

Turning to Marna and Asti, he made a formal bow, striking the butt of his spear on the sand-strewn floor as he did so. It was a peculiar action and Derin, his curiosity aroused, looked carefully at the shaft of the spear, noticing for the first time that, like his crutch, it had a heavy metal base – a base which did not match the metal of the spearhead, as though it had been added to the weapon after its completion. He was still staring at this metal base when, with an abrupt movement, Ardelan lifted the spear clear of the ground, leaving in the sand the imprint of a familiar pattern – the ancient sign of the Council – the tiny outline of a sword enclosed by a circle of stars.

Derin glanced quickly at Ardelan's face. In a flash he realized that this was no ordinary upland farmer; nor just a Captain of the Guard; Ardelan, his own father, was the tenth and secret member of the Council. Yet that wasn't all Derin understood: the pattern still visible in the sand was exactly the size and shape of the mark which he had seen in the snow when he had woken in the wood. He thought, so Ardelan was the one who followed and attacked me. But why? Why him? He felt suddenly dizzy and he leaned back against the wall and closed his eyes. When he opened them, Ardelan had almost reached the door.

'Stop!' Derin cried faintly.

Ardelan turned and looked back, quizzically.

'What is it?' he said.

But instead of asking the many questions which came crowding into his mind, Derin merely murmured:

'Nothing ... it doesn't matter.'

For one other thing was now clear to him: this strong, reserved man who stood facing him was not his father as Marna claimed; he was a total stranger.

11. The East

Once they had worked out a plan of action, there was nothing more for them to do for the rest of the day. Marna and Asti, mindful of the testing time ahead, lay down on the straw bed and went to sleep; but Derin felt too anxious to rest and he spent most of the morning roaming unhappily around the chamber.

Two things in particular worried him. The first was the mystery surrounding Ardelan. Why had he, the secret member of the Council, pretended to be his father? What had he been doing in the uplands and why had he gone to the trouble of following his supposed son into the woods and knocking him unconscious? Even more puzzling, if Marna was in league with Ardelan (as she surely had to be), why had she insisted on undertaking the hazardous journey to Iri-Nan and on bringing Derin with her? After all, Ardelan had presumably attacked Derin in order to prevent his undertaking the journey. The more Derin thought about such problems, the more convinced he became that there was some purpose behind all that had happened to him. But what was it? Did it perhaps tie in with the star-shaped emblem on the tip of the crutch he carried? And how could that purpose be accomplished if he and Marna were simply to turn around and go back to where they had come from?

Unable to make sense of his predicament, Derin stopped beside one of the window-openings and stared out over the plains. He was facing north, and that great expanse, with the woodlands reduced to a dull green line in the distance, only served to remind him of his second worry - which was how to cross such a vast open space without being recaptured. No matter how he viewed it, the task appeared impossible. Perhaps Marna had some plan of action; but she was fast asleep, lying flat on her back snoring contentedly. In any case he had vowed never to be led by her again. No, he had to think up some plan of his own.

Unfortunately, a disguise was out of the question because he could not hide his limp which would be certain to betray him – that and the soldiers' sure knowledge of where he would be headed. They knew he could not penetrate the desert regions to the west and south of Iri-Nan. And to the east lay the threat of the Grove. Therefore only one route was open to him: the one he had taken to get here, the road that led north directly towards the woodlands. There was no other way ... or was there?

All at once he realized how foolish he was being. One thing at least had been established earlier that morning: he was not one of the Witch People. He was the son of an upland farmer, and so, once free, he would try to return to his home. That, at any rate, is what the Council and the soldiers would suppose. He, too, had made the same assumption. Whereas in fact his situation was slightly different: there was an alternative open to him; a route they would never dream of his taking – along which no soldier would dare venture. It was in that direction he must go.

With the decision made, he immediately relaxed and slept soundly for the rest of the afternoon. Marna woke him just as dusk was falling.

'Come, boy,' she said, shaking him, 'the guard will be here soon.'

'And look,' Asti added, 'Craak has returned. That is a good omen.'

Derin stood up and wiped the sleep from his eyes. Perched on the broad sill of a window-opening, his night-black feathers outlined against the pale evening sky, was Craak. At a signal from Derin, he flew across the chamber and landed lightly on his shoulder.

'Welcome,' Derin said softly, ruffling the soft breast-feathers.

At the sight of Craak, Marna rubbed her hands together, an eager glint in her eyes.

'Everything is going well,' she said. 'You'll see, in a few hours from now we'll be on our way to the uplands.'

'No, Marna,' Derin replied, 'you and Asti can go that way if you please. I shall be heading for the mountains.'

'To the east!' Marna hissed at him. 'Has being cooped up in here warped your judgement? Death or at best enslavement awaits you there.'

'Not necessarily. You forget that so far the bowmen have spared me. Back there, near the woodlands, one even offered me sanctuary in the east. If my luck holds and I manage to reach the mountains alive, I should be able to make my way north using the foothills as cover, and then strike across towards the uplands later.'

There was a short silence as Marna and Asti considered his plan.

'What Derin says makes good sense,' Asti said. 'The route he suggests would be no more hazardous than trying to reach the woodlands directly.'

'Yes, but what about Krob?' Marna murmured.

She paced nervously up and down before stopping in front of Derin.

'All right,' she said, 'I agree. For once you seem to have used your brains. We'll go east and then follow the mountains. Asti can leave us when we're level with the woodlands; and we'll continue on.'

But Derin shook his head.

'This time I travel alone,' he said. 'I told you yesterday that I wouldn't follow at your heels any longer, and I meant it.'

'Ah, so that's how it is,' Marna said, smiling at him and scratching her head with one bony finger. 'Very well, from now on we'll follow at your heels. You lead; you make the decisions. What do you say to that?'

Derin hesitated.

'I'm not sure,' he said. 'If you come with me, it may be more hazardous for all of us. The Council knows you're both witches and so there's more chance of their looking for you on the eastern road.'

'I think not,' Marna countered quickly. 'We proved we're no friends of the Grove when we opposed Illam. That doesn't mean the Council trusts us; but at least they won't expect us to go east.'

Derin looked at Marna and Asti.

'We'll stay together, then,' he said. 'But we all make our own decisions; nobody decides for anyone else. Is that understood?'

Marna nodded, clearly satisfied by the agreement.

'And now,' she said, 'we must prepare ourselves. Soon it will be dark.'

They took up their agreed positions and waited in silence - Derin beside the door; Marna in the centre of the chamber; Asti on the bed. Slowly the shadows lengthened, the sky growing steadily darker, the pale pinpoints of starlight appearing one by one. Not until the room was in total darkness did they hear the tramp of footsteps on the stairs.

'Get ready,' Marna whispered.

A light showed at the bottom of the door as the footsteps stopped outside. The lock was turned, the latch lifted, and the door swung open - Derin keeping behind it so he shouldn't be seen. A voice said:

'You go in. I'll wait here, just in case they try anything.'

One of the guards stepped into the doorway and stopped.

'Where're the others?' he said suspiciously.

Marna pointed to the bed, where her cloak was thrown loosely over Asti's silent form. In the dim light it was impossible to make out exactly who was lying in the bed.

'The boy and the girl are sleeping,' she said.

Reassured, the guard advanced two further paces into the room, but still taking care to keep well back from Marna.

'Here ...' he said - and stopped dead as Marna suddenly stretched out one hand towards him.

He was now less than a pace from Derin who had drawn his dagger. Quickly he stepped from behind the door and held the point to the guard's neck.

'If you cry out,' he said to the man outside, 'your companion dies.'

It was completely dark on the landing and Derin could see nothing out there; but he heard the man edging slowly backwards.

'What do you want?' the voice asked him nervously.

'We'll harm neither of you if you come in here,' Derin said. 'My word on that. But if you try to run or give the alarm you'll both die.'

'How do I know I can trust you?' the voice asked.

Derin pressed the point against the skin of the guard's neck.

'You're wasting time,' he said impatiently. 'I give you to the count of ten and no more. One, two, three, four ...'

The other guard came shuffling reluctantly into the chamber. Instantly Marna pointed at him and he too froze in his tracks.

With a knowing smile she stepped up to the two guards who now stood quite still, their eyes vacant, their bodies transfixed.

'These two beauties won't be going anywhere for a while,' she said. 'They should stay like this for at least an hour.'

'An hour's not long,' Derin said doubtfully.

'We'll have to make the best of it,' Marna replied. 'We have no rope to tie them up with. What else can we do?'

'There is one other possibility,' Asti said quietly.

'What's that?' Marna asked.

'I could stay here and maintain the spell that binds them,' she murmured, obviously having to force herself to voice her thoughts.

'Don't talk nonsense, girl,' Marna responded abruptly. 'We'll be well clear of here before the alarm's sounded.'

She tried to grasp Asti's hand, but Asti drew back - sudden determination, like a dark shadow, passing across her features.

'No,' she said firmly, 'better that you two escape.'

'But why should you sacrifice yourself for us?' Derin asked.

'It's hard to explain,' she said hesitantly. 'Perhaps you'll understand better later. All I can tell you now is that I made a vow to Obin: I promised to bind my life to the rock that shielded the Warden's Staff. And in helping you to escape, I'm partially fulfilling that vow. At least I hope so. Now you must go.'

She pushed him gently towards Marna, who was waiting in the doorway.

'But I don't understand,' Derin said.

'Come!' Marna said urgently. 'You were the one who insisted that we make our own decisions. She's made her choice - let her stand by it.'

Marna was already clattering down the stairs.

'You're sure?' Derin asked Asti, still lingering in the doorway.

'Quite sure,' she said, waving him away.

Reluctantly he turned and followed Marna. In the long descent they met no one - only their shadows, cast by the smoky light, pursuing them down the stairwell. At the bottom they found that Ardelan, true to his word, had left the doors untended; and between them they lifted off the heavy bar and turned the two big keys in their locks. The doors opened without a sound, and one behind the other they slipped out into the cool night. They were about to steal across the square when a voice murmured:

'It would not be wise to leave the doors open.'

Derin whirled around and saw the pale face of Arith watching him from the shadows.

'What are you doing here?' he asked anxiously.

'Ardelan told me of your plan,' he answered. 'I'm here to guide you.'

'But you've already helped me once,' Derin said.

'I owe you my life,' Arith said solemnly, 'and that debt will not be repaid until you are beyond the reach of the Council. As for the old woman, she may come with us or go her own way, as she chooses.'

'It isn't often the plains folk help anyone,' Marna said with a chuckle, 'and I'll not miss this opportunity.'

Having pulled the big doors closed, Arith led them around the side of the Citadel and into a narrow alleyway.

'The city gates close at the ninth hour,' he whispered, 'so we have no time to lose.'

In single file, with Arith leading, they hurried through the twisting streets. The stone paving jarred Derin's shoulder, the metal tip of the crutch ringing out a staccato beat as he planted it down after each step. Arith, familiar with the sounds of the city, seemed always to sense any movement ahead; and he warned them in good time, drawing them into some shadowy doorway while the danger passed. Even so, they were relieved to reach the great arched opening in the outer wall. At this time of night little traffic was passing through and the four guards stood sleepily at their posts.

'How do we get past them unnoticed?' Derin whispered.

'Leave that to me,' Arith said with a smile, and produced a stone bottle from beneath his tunic. 'While I keep them occupied, sneak through on the side furthest from the flares. And wait for me outside.'

With a nonchalant air, he walked slowly towards the guards.

'Any trouble tonight?' he called out.

One of the guards glanced up, blinking sleepily.

'Quiet as a mouse, Arith,' he said gruffly.

'Then a drop of this won't do you any harm,' Arith said, flourishing the bottle.

The guards gathered round him, eagerly waiting their turn for a pull at the bottle. While they were so engaged Marna and Derin crept past them, keeping as far from the lights as possible, Derin using the side wall instead of the crutch to support him.

'We did it,' he said with relief as they emerged onto the plain.

'Hush!' Marna whispered, and drew him into the shadow of the wall.

They didn't have long to wait. Arith soon appeared beside them and pointed to the north-west.

'There's a little-used path over there,' he said. 'We'll follow it and cut back to the northern road later.'

'We're not heading north,' Derin replied. 'From here, we strike east, towards the mountains.'

'East!' Arith said, surprised, and he looked narrowly at Marna. 'Are you asking me to guide you to the enemies of the plains?'

Derin shook his head and briefly explained their reason for choosing the eastern road. Arith listened attentively and finally nodded.

'One thing is certain,' he said, 'our chances of reaching the woodlands by the northern route would not be great. As for the mountains, only you can assess the danger that awaits you there. But if that's the way you choose, I'll take you as far as I'm able to.'

Behind them the guards began closing the heavy gates for the night. There was a squealing of hinges and a clang of metal; and under cover of the noise and darkness the three fugitives skirted the wall and stole noiselessly along a path which led directly towards the eastern road.

A cool breeze was blowing, ruffling the wheat on either side of the path and carrying with it the smell of damp earth.

'There'll be rain before long,' Marna warned them.

And soon after they joined the main road a light drizzle began to fall. It grew steadily harder as the night wore on, until soon the dusty surface of the road had grown into a slick of soft mud on which Derin had to struggle to keep his feet.

'Our luck continues to hold,' Arith said. 'There will be few travellers abroad in weather like this.'

Marna slipped and nearly fell.

'You plains people have a funny idea of luck,' she grumbled.

But what Arith said was true: except for the occasional patrol nobody passed them. Fortunately the soldiers caused them no trouble: their heavy footsteps were clearly audible above the soft rustle of the rain, giving them ample time to take refuge in the ditch beside the road.

By morning they were wet and tired; but, far more important, they had covered many miles. Arith, who knew the road well, was sure they were more than half way to the border garrison.

'One more night,' he promised them, 'and you should be safely beyond the reach of the Council.'

But Marna, who had been grumbling since the rain began, said:

'It's the day ahead that worries me. What do you expect us to do? Hide somewhere out there in the wet furrows?'

'Don't worry about that,' Arith assured her. 'I'll arrange something.'

The dim light of early dawn gradually began to break through the darkness and rain. Directly ahead, but still some way off, they could make out the grey outline of the foothills - with the tops of the mountains hidden by low cloud.

'We'll turn off here,' Arith said, and led them along a bumpy track to a lone farmhouse.

It was still in darkness and Arith had to knock for some time before a man came to the door. He was tall and middle-aged, with a gaunt face that looked as though it had been dried by years of hot summer wind. He seemed to know Arith, but peered suspiciously at Marna and Derin. He seemed alarmed most of all by the sight of Craak who, wet and bedraggled, still clung to Derin's shoulder.

'What's this, then?' he said, pointing an accusing finger at Derin and the bird. 'It's witches, is it?'

Arith merely laughed.

'That's what they look like, right enough,' he replied, and then lowered his voice to a whisper: 'In fact they're plains folk, like you and me - spies for the Council. My job is to escort them to the border and help them slip across.'

A faint expression of excitement appeared on the man's dried-up face.

'Secret, is it?' he said.

'Yes, a plot to defeat the Grove,' Arith said, winking at the man. 'Nobody must know about it. We need a place to hide during the day.'

'There's always room here for enemies of the Grove,' the man said, and took them to the kitchen where he built up the fire that had been smouldering all night.

There they dried out their clothes and ate the hot food he prepared for them. Then they followed him to the barn and, burrowing into a heap of dry straw, slept soundly throughout the day.

The man roused them as dusk was setting in; and after another meal they again set out, their host escorting them as far as the road.

'Many thanks,' Derin said, feeling genuinely grateful to him.

'I don't begrudge it,' the man replied, 'just as long as it helps us beat the Grove.'

'Oh we'll beat them all right,' Marna said, cheerful again now that she was warm and well fed, 'don't you worry about that.'

In the gathering darkness they hurried along the road, all three of them aware that by now the news of their escape would be filtering through to the outer regions of the plain.

'We must be extra careful from here on,' Arith warned them. 'As we get closer to the outer garrison we can expect to run into road checks.'

In spite of his warning, nothing happened until shortly before midnight. They had not yet reached the foothills, but for the first time since leaving Iri-Nan the road began to rise slightly. After the miles of flatness the slight gradient felt like a steep hill and Marna was soon grumbling.

'It's all right for you young ones . . .' she was saying.

But she was interrupted by Craak who let out a low warning cry.

'What is it?' Derin whispered.

Arith peered into the darkness ahead.

'Some kind of road check, most likely,' he said.

He led them off the road, down in amongst the tender blades of young wheat. After the rain of the previous night the ground was soft underfoot and they found it heavy going. Marna complained more than ever; yet Arith insisted on their making a detour of almost half a mile before rejoining the road. Now, although they didn't slacken their pace, they were more watchful - and with due cause, for less than an hour later they were again forced to take to the fields. This time they actually saw the patrol. In creeping quietly through the darkness, they very nearly blundered into the soldiers' camp and had to withdraw quickly, tripping over each other's feet in their haste.

From then on they ran into one obstacle after another, and soon they were spending more time making detours than travelling on the road.

'It's no good,' Arith said finally, 'we'll have to leave the road altogether and stay in the fields. It's our only hope of getting through.'

Reluctantly, they crossed the ditch and began tramping across the soggy furrows, the young wheat swishing against their legs. With the sky still overcast they had only the vaguest sense of direction, their guides being the wind and the slope of the land. Soon they came to the steepest hill they had encountered. As they climbed, they began to discern a faint glow somewhere near the top; and when they neared the crest they crouched low and peered cautiously into the slight hollow beyond. They saw at once what had caused the unnatural light: in the shallow valley below them was a large encampment of soldiers from Iri-Nan - rank after rank of white tents surrounded by a circle of small fires.

'It must be the outer garrison,' Arith whispered.

'Then you had better turn back,' Derin replied. 'It will be dangerous for you to go any further. From now on we'll find our own way.'

Arith waved the suggestion aside.

'I'll see you safely into the foothills,' he said.

Warily, they began to circle the encampment. More than once Craak croaked softly in Derin's ear, always just in time to warn them of some nearby sentry; and it soon seemed likely that they would succeed in creeping undetected through the lines. But with the encampment immediately behind them, Craak suddenly let out a peculiarly urgent cry. They turned aside as usual, only to run straight into another sentry, his weather-worn armour invisible against the dark background.

By sheer coincidence he actually knew Arith, and for a moment he stood staring at him, confused, unable to grasp what was happening.

'Arith!' he said, surprised. 'What are you doing ... and who are these ...?'

The truth dawned on him abruptly, and with a quick defensive movement he drew his sword and stepped back, barring their way.

'Let us pass,' Arith said quietly. 'We mean you no harm.'

'No harm!' the soldier said accusingly, 'when you're helping the enemies of the plain?'

Before Arith could reply, he lunged directly at Derin.

'Death to all witches!' he snarled as he thrust forward with his sword.

Derin deflected the blow with the crutch, the steel giving out a high ringing note as it glanced off the hardened wood. Moving with surprising speed, the soldier raised his sword for a second blow. But Arith stepped between them, parrying the attack with his own sword.

'That's enough!' he said warningly. 'You have to listen ...'

He broke off as the soldier pushed him away and lunged this time at Marna. Undefended as she was, the blade would probably have killed her if it hadn't been for Arith. Caught up in the heat of the moment, he swung his sword, the sharp edge cutting through the soldier's light body armour and sinking into his ribs. Groaning softly, he slumped to his knees and, with a last incredulous look at Arith, fell unconscious to the ground.

'The fool!' Marna said, staring down at the prostrate figure.

But for the second time since their arrival on the plains, Arith struck her across the mouth, sending her staggering off into the shadows.

'Be silent, witch!' he said. 'He was worth a hundred of the like of you.'

Mumbling curses to herself, Marna sprang back towards him, obviously intent on transfixing him with a spell. But Derin pushed the shaft of the crutch directly in her path and stopped her.

'Enough,' he said quietly.

And kneeling down beside the wounded man, he examined his injury and listened for his heartbeat.

'He's still alive,' he said to Arith. 'If you take him back to the camp now, he'll probably be all right.'

Arith shook his head sadly.

'For me there can be no going back,' he said. 'I've turned against one of my own people; there's no place for me on the plains any more.'

'You can't just leave the man here to die,' Derin protested.

'I shan't do that,' he replied. 'Carry on for another hundred paces and then wait for me. I'll be with you shortly.'

They walked away into the darkness and waited. From the spot they had just left came cries of help from Arith. These were answered by the cries of other sentries posted elsewhere on the hillside and by the sound of hasty footsteps. A light flared in the darkness, and then another; and Marna, who was growing more nervous with each passing second, plucked impatiently at Derin's sleeve.

'It's dangerous to wait here any longer,' she said.

Derin too was frightened of being discovered and began edging away; but a faint murmur from Craak made him turn, and to his relief Arith appeared out of the shadows.

'Come,' he said, 'they'll soon be up here looking for us. We must get to the foothills quickly - they'll not dare search for us there.'

They hurried up the slope, pausing only briefly to glance back at the bobbing cluster of lights that had formed around the injured man.

'You belong down there, with your own people,' Marna said severely. 'There's still time for you to circle back behind the lines. Nobody would guess your part in all this.'

'I have no need of your advice, witch,' Arith replied. 'What is betrayal to you but a word? To me it is much more. I have betrayed my allegiance and from now on my road lies elsewhere.'

'Dressed as you are, as a soldier of the plains,' Marna warned him, 'this road will be particularly dangerous to you.'

'All roads are dangerous in times of war,' he said shortly.

And with a last backward look of regret, he led the way over the rise, the three of them plunging down into the unrelieved darkness beyond.

The land became ever more hilly after that - with steep rises, followed by narrow plateaus or hollows which immediately gave way to yet steeper hills. They pushed on, barely speaking, stopping only when Marna was forced to rest, her chest wheezing as she lay back fighting for breath. Derin once suggested that they camp for the remainder of the night, but she turned on him so fiercely that he didn't mention the idea again.

'Would you have me come all this way only to get caught?' she grumbled.

And struggling to her feet, she staggered off into the night.

By morning they were deep into the foothills and already the air was growing thin and chill. Before them, the hills, dimly visible in the dawn light, rose up and up, forming into lofty peaks that disappeared into the high cloud. As the light grew stronger, the cloud dissolved, revealing the tips of the highest peaks, the whole jagged ridge of the mountain chain outlined in gold by the rising sun.

Now, for the first time in many hours, they were able to stop and look around them. They found themselves in a colourless, almost lifeless world of grey, with only a few stunted bushes growing on the long shale slopes or in amongst the heavy boulders that had settled in the hollows.

'The price of freedom and power,' Marna said, pointing a crooked finger at the grey landscape and cackling with mirthless laughter.

'Just be quiet for a minute,' Derin cautioned her, for Craak had suddenly grown restless, moving his weight from one foot to the other, his black beak tapping gently at Derin's cheek as a sign of warning.

But Marna was not to be silenced so easily.

'Do you know how Krob sees all this?' she went on. 'As a garden, in which trees flourish, roses bloom, and birds sing their endless songs of spring. These barren hills are invisible to him. And can you guess why? Because he's blind. The Staff has burned out his sight; the Staff alone sustains both him and his bowmen; and without it he would be a hollow-eyed skull, his dreams of Eden vanished; a poor scarecrow blundering around in the darkness of his own withered mind.'

'Craak,' the bird whispered, his beady eye fixed on the nearest ridge.

'Listen!' Derin said urgently.

But still Marna only smiled – a strange smile which might almost have been an expression of triumph.

'It's too late for caution,' she said. 'Did you think we could creep through these regions unnoticed? They are already waiting for us. Look!'

She pointed upwards, towards the ridge, and gradually, in the growing light of morning, a long line of armed figures became visible. They were all dressed differently: men and women from the uplands and the woodlands; even a few taller, blond-haired figures from the plain. But all had one thing in common: their eyes were dull and without curiosity. They lacked the totally dead gaze of the bowmen; none the less, something had gone out of them, some spark of life.

'Who are they?' Derin whispered.

'They are the advance rank of Krob's legions,' Marna answered.

'Then they'll have to buy our lives dearly,' Arith said, reaching for his sword.

Before he could draw it, an arrow sped down from the ridge and buried itself in his upper arm. With a cry of pain he fell back.

'You're as empty-headed as this boy,' Marna said reprovingly. 'Do you think you can fight the whole world?'

And advancing slowly up the slope, she spread her arms wide, showing clearly that she was unarmed.

'We come in peace,' she called. 'We are fugitives from the plains. All we ask is a safe passage through the mountains.'

Nobody answered her. Slowly, as silently as they had appeared, the line of watchful figures melted back behind the ridge.

Derin meanwhile had knelt beside Arith. Grasping the shaft of the arrow, he tried to pull it free; but the point was barbed and wouldn't budge - his efforts producing only a stifled gasp of pain from Arith. And so he took out his dagger and cut through the shaft just where it entered the skin.

'That's the best I can do,' he said, tossing the long-feathered shaft aside. 'At least now the point won't move and give you pain as you walk.'

Marna was busy tearing a strip of cloth from her cloak.

'Bind the arm with this,' she said. 'It will serve until we have a chance to cut the head free and clean the wound.'

His arm roughly bandaged, Arith rose to his feet. His face was paler than usual, but otherwise he appeared well enough and ready to go on.

With the top of the sun peering above the lower peaks, they climbed up towards the ridge. Nobody was waiting for them on the far side, the long grey slopes deserted. Relieved, they pressed on, pushing ever deeper into the mountains. From time to time they spied figures watching from the heights, but no further attempt was made to bar their way.

By mid morning they were high above the plains: the wheatlands stretched beneath them like smooth green cloth; the walls of Iri-Nan, grown vague and indistinct, wavering slightly in the far distance.

'Isn't it time we turned towards the north?' Derin said.

'Here is as good a place as any,' Marna said wearily.

They rested for a few minutes and then changed direction, following the line of the mountain range, keeping the sun on their right. They had not gone very far, however, when a bowman suddenly stepped out from behind a huge boulder directly in their path. In one pale hand he held a bow; with the other he pointed to the almost sheer slopes of the mountains.

'Your way lies towards the east,' he said in a ghostly whisper, his dead eyes fixed upon them.

'No,' Arith said quickly, 'we are heading for the north.'

The thin hand swung slowly round until it pointed directly at him.

'You alone may pass,' he said to Arith. 'The other two must continue on as before.'

To Derin's surprise, Arith nodded in agreement. Turning to his companions, he said:

'I have repaid my debt. I've brought you safely beyond the reach of the Council. Now it seems our ways must part.'

And after bowing to them both, he strode off towards the north. But just as he was passing the bowman, he suddenly whipped out his sword and swung it with all his might at the deathly figure beside him, the blade cutting through the folds of the cloak and biting deeply into the skeletal body beneath. Without a sound, the bowman seemed almost to fold in two, his frail body broken by the terrible blow; and as his black unseeing eyes closed for the last time, he slid slowly to the ground.

Arith, sword in hand, stood over his fallen victim.

'Did he think that I would forget so easily,' he said, his voice trembling with anger, 'that I would miss a chance to avenge all the men shot down by these creatures?'

'Take care, Arith!' Marna called out to him.

At the same instant Craak launched himself into the air. Yet both the bird's swift flight and Marna's cry of warning came too late. Like a sinister coil of mist, the black vapour issued from the nostrils and mouth of the corpse, swirling towards Arith and enveloping his head. With a scream of agony, he spun around and fell, striking his helmeted head repeatedly against the rocky slope in a frantic attempt to expel the dark force that had lodged itself within him.

'Arith!' Derin cried out, and would have run to his aid had Marna not prevented him by throwing her bony arms around his body.

'You can do nothing!' she hissed at him.

He tried to tear himself free, but already Arith had ceased to struggle. He lay quite still for a full minute; and then very slowly rose to his feet, his back towards his companions.

'Are you all right?' Derin called out.

He didn't answer. He merely turned towards them. And Derin, to his dismay, found himself staring into the blank, lustreless eyes of one of the walking dead.

12. The Place of the Circle

To Derin, the sunlit day seemed to have grown noticeably darker.

'Arith!' he said fearfully. 'Can you hear me?'

The dead eyes continued to stare back at him and he glanced quickly away, knowing from experience what might happen if he met that blank gaze.

'Arith,' he said again, 'answer me!'

A spasm passed across Arith's features as a brief struggle took place within him. That was the last show of resistance, and once again his face became an expressionless mask totally devoid of sense or feeling.

'You're wasting your time,' Marna said quietly. 'Krob has taken him.'

'Surely there's something we can do!' Derin said desperately. 'We can't just leave him here like this.'

'I don't think there's any question of our leaving him,' Marna replied.

Her meaning soon became clear, for Arith had already raised his hand and pointed towards the mountain peaks. In the same ghostly whisper as the bowman he had just killed, he said:

'You will continue towards the east. The Grove awaits you.'

'No,' Derin said, 'we travel north. Can't you remember even that?'

With slow deliberate movements Arith stooped over the fallen bowman, plucked the bow from his hand, and pulled a thin quiver of arrows from the folds of his cloak. Notching one of the arrows onto the string, he bent the bow and pointed it directly at Derin.

'The Grove will not be denied,' he rasped out.

But still Derin didn't move.

'Your threats won't change my mind, Arith,' he said, 'because I don't believe you'll kill me. Not you.'

'You aren't speaking to Arith, child,' Marna warned him. 'You are facing one of Krob's creatures.'

'Then I still have nothing to fear,' he said. 'They've protected me so far. Why should they change now?'

He took a step forward. But the moment he moved, Arith swung the bow around and pointed it at Marna.

'Unless you obey, the witch will die,' he said in the same flat emotionless voice.

Derin looked at Marna.

'He means it,' she said, a wry smile twisting her withered lips.

'But what's the point of our going to the Grove?' he burst out, feeling trapped between two forces, neither of which he fully understood.

'My master awaits you,' Arith intoned.

The knuckles of his left hand were growing white with the effort of holding the bow bent. Yet still Derin hesitated, loth to become a pawn once more in this mysterious game which he could not fathom.

'It was bad enough following at your heels,' he said angrily to Marna. 'Must I now be at Krob's beck and call?'

'You are the one who wanted to be free,' Marna reminded him. 'Didn't you realize that all we can ever hope for is the freedom to choose? And that you have always had. So come, boy, make your decision.'

Her voice was even and steady, betraying no sign of fear.

'Don't you even care about your own life?' he said, exasperated by her. 'Are you too proud to plead?'

'The time for pleading is past,' she answered, her eyes fixed on the arrow aimed at her throat. 'Now is the time for sifting our friends from our enemies, our loves from our hatreds, our trust from our fear.'

With a muttered curse, Derin turned towards the mountains.

'Spare her,' he said bitterly. 'I accept your bargain: her life for my freedom.'

Beside him, he heard Marna chuckle to herself.

'Ah, that hurt, I know,' she said. 'To give up your liberty for an old witch who cares for no one but herself - that's hard.'

'What else could I do?' he retorted. 'Did you expect me to stand by and see you killed? I'd have done the same for any living creature.'

'What difference does that make?' she said, laughing openly at him. 'I still call it a victory of the heart. And oh, how that will upset Krob. He won't approve at all. Nor of you, my beautiful,' she added, ruffling the breast-feathers of Craak who had returned to Derin's shoulder.

'I care no more for Krob's approval than I do for yours,' Derin said.

'Brave words,' Marna replied. 'We'll see if you have actions to fit them.'

And with a casual flick of her tattered cloak, she began to scramble up the rocky slope.

Less than an hour later they reached a small mountain lake not much bigger than a village pond. It was the first water they had seen since entering the mountains and they drank deeply. Arith, who had continued to follow them, stood aloof, apparently unmoved by such things as hunger and thirst. As soon as they had drunk their fill, he said:

'It has been decided that you will rest here and gather your strength for the journey ahead.'

They both welcomed the news: they had been walking for sixteen hours and were bone weary. Marna lay down exactly where she was and went straight to sleep. Derin looked suspiciously at the silent figure of Arith, wondering whether it was safe to close his eyes, but a soft cry from Craak reassured him and he too lay down and fell asleep.

Arith woke them late in the afternoon.

'It is time,' was all he said.

Already, at such an altitude, the air was crisp and frosty. The slopes all about them were now completely barren, with not so much as a sprig of green to be seen anywhere. Even the slightest hollow was touched with the purple shadows of evening; while above them the towering peaks, stained a dusky yellow by the setting sun, showed like the jagged, broken stumps of teeth in some giant's mouth. Derin shuddered and rose hastily to his feet. In that ominous evening light he had the feeling that he was journeying to his death, and that if he had any sense he would ignore Arith's threats and flee back down the mountainside.

'A pretty place, isn't it?' Marna said with a cackle of laughter. 'Consider what a fool Krob must be to give his life for this. But then, as I told you, he can't see it. Blind as these sightless rocks, he is, fondly imagining that each speck of dust is a rose in bloom, that the ashy feel of the dry air upon his tongue is the taste of heaven.'

To Derin's amazement she seemed untroubled by her surroundings or by the daunting prospect of meeting the keeper of the Staff. All the impatience and ill humour she had shown on the plains had left her. Grasping the shaft of Derin's crutch, she pulled herself upright, grumbling light-heartedly about her stiff joints and worn-out old bones.

'It is I who should have the stick,' she said with a laugh, 'not a young scatterbrained boy. Stout of limb and soft of brain, that's you.'

Derin said nothing, noticing only how Arith grew momentarily tense as Marna placed her hands upon the crutch. That moment past, he pointed to a high narrow pass between two peaks.

'The place of the Circle,' he said.

Derin looked up and saw not only the pass but, on a nearby ridge, a line of men and women, all of them armed with bows, gazing down. Higher up, he could make out smaller groups or lone sentinels, their heads and shoulders silhouetted against the darkening sky.

'What are they doing there?' Derin asked.

'They're waiting for Krob to tell them to march on the plains,' Marna replied. 'They think of nothing but the taking of Iri-Nan – their memories of the past forgotten. Such is the power of the Staff.'

'I've also forgotten the past,' Derin said quietly. 'Am I perhaps becoming like them?'

'You?' Marna said with a laugh. 'What an idea! Why, you're as different from these folk as' – she groped for a comparison – 'as I am from this husk of Arith. No, child, with or without your memories you retain the freedom to think and choose – as you'll find out soon enough.'

'What do you mean by that?' Derin asked.

But she refused to answer, gathering her cloak about her as protection from the cold and lifting her face resolutely towards the pass.

As the sun sank below the flat horizon, they began the last and most difficult part of the climb. In the rarefied air it was harder than ever to labour up the steep slopes and they stopped frequently, gasping for breath, their faces damp with sweat in spite of the icy atmosphere. At times the slope became a sheer, vertical wall of rock, and then they had to climb hand over hand up swinging chain ladders, the bare metal making their fingers ache with cold. On the steeper parts of the journey Craak would fly off into the night, relieving Derin of the burden of his weight. But he always returned, croaking belligerently at the zombie-like figure of Arith that continued to follow them.

For Derin, probably the most testing part of that night's journey was the feeling of not knowing where he was. Although the stars shone bright and clear in the crisp mountain air, their light alone was not sufficient to see beyond the immediate surroundings; and so, as the long hours slowly passed without his once catching a glimpse of the pass above them, he began to feel that the mountain slope was endless, rising up for ever, their ultimate, impossible destination the stars themselves.

It was Marna who finally dispelled this feeling. They had reached another chain ladder and were catching their breath before they began the climb. Craak, who usually left Derin's shoulder at such times, fluttered his wings as though in preparation for flight, but at the last moment he changed his mind and settled himself once again.

'See, the bird grows unwilling to leave you,' Marna said. 'That means the pass must be near.'

They climbed the ladder in silence and, at the top, while they were resting briefly, Derin noticed how the sky was lightening; and there, immediately above them, was the neck of the pass itself, a U-shaped area of grey showing against the general blackness.

From then on the dawn advanced rapidly - the stars disappearing; the surrounding rocks, glittering with frost, emerging from the gloom. Long before the sun had risen they had reached the pass, a narrow defile between glistening walls of stone. Derin now saw that it didn't lead through the range as he'd expected: instead, it sloped up towards a rocky plateau which lay just below the level of the peaks. In the very centre of this plateau, shadowed by the mountains and facing out across the plains, was a long white building; and it was towards this that they now climbed.

At a distance, the building looked plain and unadorned. But as they drew nearer, emerging from the pass onto the flat expanse of rock, Derin noticed something which made him stop instantly. In the middle of the building was a large wooden door, and above the door, painted in blue and gold, was a ten-pointed star surrounded by a circle - exactly the same design as that engraved on the metal tip of the crutch.

He turned questioningly to Marna.

'What is the meaning of that pattern?' he asked her.

She gave him a strangely knowing glance.

'I'm surprised you haven't guessed before now,' she said. 'It is the sign of the sacred Circle, the ancient emblem of the Grove.'

'Then why ...?' he began.

But she silenced him with a nervous movement of her hand.

'What do reasons matter any longer?' she said as they walked on. 'Krob is the master of all reasons and I cannot hope to match him in argument. Only a warm and trusting heart can protect us now. Therefore to the heart within you I say: Remain watchful and at the ready. Nothing else matters in this high and lonely place.'

Marna's answer mystified Derin. Yet there was a finality about her tone which discouraged further questions and he looked once more at the design over the door. There was no doubt that it was identical to the pattern he had carried with him all the way from the uplands. And as he gazed at it, he began for the first time to discern some suggestion of a purpose behind all that had happened. Before he could clearly formulate his own suspicions, however, they arrived at the building.

As though prompted by some inner compulsion, Derin reached out in order to strike the heavy wooden door with the crutch. But Marna quickly intervened.

'No,' she said firmly, pushing the crutch aside and rapping on the door with her bare knuckles.

They didn't have long to wait. The door was soon opened by an old woman in flowing blue robes. Like the people they had seen on the ridge the previous day, her eyes were dull and lacking in any inner vitality, as though she had been drugged. But at the sight of Marna and Derin a spark of life and vigour appeared momentarily in her face.

'You must leave here!' she whispered urgently. 'This is no place...'

'Silence!'

The order came from Arith, his hoarse voice unusually loud and authoritative.

'You will keep them here until sunset,' he commanded. 'When the sun touches the horizon, I shall return and conduct them to the Grove.'

The vitality immediately left the old woman's face, replaced once more by the dull, almost drugged expression.

Having ushered Marna and Derin inside, she led them along the passage to a large kitchen. There they found a group of other old people dressed in blue robes. They too showed some signs of interest at the first sight of the newcomers; but their interest was short-lived.

'These are Krob's prisoners,' the old woman informed them.

And straight away the light went out of their eyes and they sank back in their chairs or busied themselves preparing the morning meal.

Marna, in spite of her fatigue, seemed not to have lost her good humour of the previous evening. With a sly grin at Derin, she said:

'Prisoners we may be, but it's they who'll wait on us. You'll see.'

Sure enough, minutes later the old people placed two steaming bowls of food in front of them. Marna, spoon in hand, breathed in the appetizing smell, a look of contentment on her face. And more than ever Derin wondered why it was she appeared so unconcerned. This, surely, was the very place she should have feared most; yet never had she been more relaxed, as though she hadn't a care in the world. With the spoon still poised above the bowl, she took another deep, pleasurable breath.

'Who needs reasons,' she said, harking back to their earlier conversation, 'when there are delicious smells like this in the world?

They speak to the heart. The heart, Derin,' she repeated, rapping the handle of the spoon on the table, 'the one place to which Krob cannot penetrate. A place of warmth and love he is too blind to see. Remember that, boy.'

And with her hair falling like a soft grey fountain around the bowl, she began to eat with great relish, filling her mouth almost to bursting and murmuring to herself with pleasure.

Derin, for all his hunger, ate more slowly, as mystified by her present attitude as he had ever been.

'Come, child,' she said cheerfully, calling for her bowl to be refilled, 'feed the warmth inside you. Without good food, friendship, and trust, the warmth will die. Feed it while you have the chance. You won't regret it, not when Krob's icy power reaches out and touches you.'

But although he too was hungry, he couldn't follow her advice. It was true what she said: there was an iciness about this place which probed at his very heart, robbing him of his appetite, so that after a dozen mouthfuls he pushed the bowl aside. Then, sitting hunched up with cold, he watched as Marna finished her second bowlful and licked the last morsels from her spoon.

'Aah,' she sighed, her sunken cheeks flushed strangely red, her eyes sparkling with enjoyment, 'that was good.'

She leaned back and surveyed the room, beaming at the old people who sat and stared dully at the fire.

'Look at them,' she said loudly, her voice portraying the same irresistible cheerfulness, 'not a smile amongst them. A typical example of Krob's handiwork.'

'Hush!' Derin whispered, 'they'll hear you.'

'No, they hear little or nothing now,' she said. 'They've become a part of Krob - all their former gaiety, all their power, stripped from them.'

'Their power?' Derin took her up. 'Who were they, then?'

'Oh, I'd forgotten,' she said, 'you'd have no way of knowing. They were once the elders of the Circle - guardians of the Grove - keepers of the peace - leaders of the Witch People.'

Derin rose abruptly to his feet.

'The Circle!' he said. 'Reduced to this! And you make a joke about it! Isn't there anything you take seriously?'

'Ah, yes,' she replied light-heartedly, 'a soft, warm bed, for instance, there's something I take seriously.'

'A bed!' he burst out, increasingly irritated by her. 'How can you think of anything as trivial as that at a time like this?'

'What else is there to think about when you're tired?' she countered.

He was about to answer her angrily, but she prevented him, wagging her finger under his nose.

'Be careful, Derin,' she cautioned him, still with a sly smile on her face, 'you're beginning to react like Krob. Krob the unlaughing – or better still, Krob the sleepless one, so ever-vigilant that he has forgotten the simple pleasures upon which life is founded. Well, I thank heaven we haven't.' She stood up and yawned. 'In fact I suggest we show Krob exactly what he's missing.'

Stepping away from the table, she signalled to the old woman who had brought them into the house.

'Where are we to spend the daylight hours?' she asked.

The old woman led them down the same passage to a large high-ceilinged room with clean white walls and a white marble floor. In each of the corners opposite the door, separated only by a broad window, were two beds piled high with soft woollen rugs.

'Ask yourself now who the true prisoner is in this lofty place,' Marna said, 'Krob or us?'

And with a chuckle of satisfaction she lay down, fully clothed as she was, and pulled one of the blankets up to her chin.

'How can you lie down and sleep?' Derin said impatiently.

But the only answer he received was a loud snore.

With a resigned shrug, he lifted Craak from his shoulder and placed the bird gently on the window sill. Then he too lay down and covered himself with a rug. It felt cosy and soft, yet somehow it failed to warm him. There was something about the house which chilled him to the bone and he continued to shiver as he had done in the warm kitchen.

How long he lay there shivering and wide awake he had no idea. Thankfully the fatigue following the long climb finally prevailed and he dropped into a light sleep. But even then he could not completely escape the biting cold: he dreamed of a freezing mountainside, the frost glittering faintly in the starlight, the stars themselves like gleaming snowflakes that tumbled slowly down and brushed icily, almost death-like, against his lips.

He stirred once, in the early afternoon, and pulled more rugs over him. Yet when he drifted back into sleep the dream immediately returned. Except that now the scene was not deserted: on every ridge, on the top of every boulder, were the many men and women he had seen during his climb from the plains, all of them watching him, their unquestioning eyes containing nothing but a reflection of the ice-cold starry night.

He awoke from the dream shivering and unhappy, aware of Craak anxiously watching him from the window sill. The moment he sat up, the bird hopped down onto his shoulder, pressing soft dark feathers comfortingly against his cheek. To his surprise, he saw that it was already early evening, with the last of the sunshine flooding the room, bathing the walls and floor in a golden light. Swinging himself off the bed, he stood before the window, allowing the sunlight to wash over his face and chest. Amazingly, it succeeded where the rugs had failed, and within minutes the cold left him.

'Store up the sun while you can,' Marna murmured approvingly, 'and set it against the chill of the Grove.

She climbed stiffly from the bed and put her arm around his shoulders, an odd mixture of sadness and contentment showing on her face.

'Back there in the uplands,' she said quietly, 'when we met in the farmhouse, I failed to give you the customary kiss of greeting. I was too cautious by far, and now it's too late to undo that wrong. Therefore we must both be satisfied with a kiss of farewell.'

And she put her withered lips to his forehead and afterwards to each of his cheeks. Then, before he could recover from his surprise, she led him out of the room and down the long passage.

The sun, like an orange and gold ball, was just touching the horizon when they opened the front door. Outside on the plateau, waiting for them, was the man they had once known as Arith.

'Krob is waiting,' he said in his ghostly voice.

'Never fear,' Marna said, winking broadly at Derin, as though the whole thing were a game, 'we shan't disappoint him.'

With Derin's hand firmly in her own, she followed the tall figure of Arith across the plateau - not this time towards the pass, but to a point slightly to the left.

Derin feared for a moment that they were being taken to their death, for, as he had noticed that morning, most of the plateau ended abruptly in a sheer precipice which plunged hundreds of feet straight down to the slopes below. But when he reached the edge, he found that at this one particular point there was a rocky staircase leading down to a circular dish of rock that jutted out into space. Over thousands of years the wind had filled the shallow dish with fine dust and minute flakes of rock, gradually building up a thin covering of soil. It was in this soil that the trees of the Grove - tiny seeds originally, also carried by the wind - had taken root and grown.

In his imagination Derin had pictured them as towering giants. But what he found himself staring at was a circle of ten gnarled and twisted shapes, so stunted by the harsh climate that even in the uplands they would have been considered no more than large bushes. The truly amazing thing about them, as he now realized, was that they had survived at all in such conditions. That in itself was almost a miracle - the simple fact of their existence the only proof necessary of the great power contained within them.

Yet there was also one outward, man-made proof of that power. Within the circle of trees another circle had been constructed: a round slab of blue-veined marble on which was drawn a large ten-pointed star of gold. Now, in the dazzling light of sunset, with the round ball of the sun half-eclipsed by the horizon, the stone slab and its glittering star appeared to be empty. But as Derin and Marna, at Arith's direction, descended the staircase, they saw that the elders of the Circle had each taken up a position at one of the points of the star, the colour of their robes merging with the blue tints of the marble. They stood perfectly still, staring before them with unseeing eyes, as unresponsive as the trees themselves. Not even an unexpected flash of brilliance from somewhere within the circle was able to attract their attention. It seemed to come from some kind of crystal which was reflecting the rays of the sinking sun. For a moment the object was hidden by the very intensity of the light shining through it. Then, as Derin and Marna reached the bottom step, they saw what it was - a solid piece of crystalline glass in which was embedded the sword they had discovered in the attic. There was no mistaking it: its ancient design and the pattern on the scabbard, showing clearly through the glass, could have belonged to no other weapon.

'The Sword of the Kings!' Derin said miserably.

Suddenly he felt close to despair, for this at least was his doing: the Sword, the only hope of the plains, placed in Krob's hands through his foolish negligence.

But Marna remained as cheerfully unconcerned as ever.

'What does it matter?' she said, giving Derin's arm a comforting squeeze. 'Look, child, the Circle is still open. Even Krob's great power has failed to complete it.'

She pointed to the tenth point of the star, which remained vacant, and at the same time she reached out and lifted Craak from Derin's shoulder. The bird didn't hesitate. Spreading his powerful wings, he flew straight between the trees towards the tenth golden point. Upon landing he let out a single cry, half of defiance, half of grief:

'Craak!'

As its echo died away, the upper rim of the sun plunged below the horizon. And at that precise moment a figure emerged from the shadow of the trees and walked slowly towards the centre of the Circle.

13. Krob

As with the trees of the Grove, Krob was nothing like Derin's mental picture of him. Asti had spoken of a withdrawn kind of person, someone capable of murdering whoever stood in his way; and Derin had imagined him as large and surly, almost brutish. Yet nothing could have been further from the truth - or so it seemed. For the man facing them in the twilight was young and slightly built, with an open, fresh face that appeared incapable of cruelty and harshness. Compared with Marna's ravaged features, he was the image of youth and innocence. Only one thing belied that impression: the skin around his eyes was worn and discoloured, as though bruised or prematurely aged.

Like the old people around him, he was dressed in blue, though the material of his long flowing robes also contained glittering threads of gold. And whereas the members of the Circle were empty-handed, he carried a short Staff made from the same wood as the ancient trees of the Grove.

'You are welcome,' he said, speaking pointedly to Derin.

He bowed formally, striking the Staff gently on the marble paving. The wood glowed slightly as he did so, and Derin felt Marna wince and stagger back. But she recovered quickly and walked between the trees to the edge of the Circle. She was smiling and relaxed, as she had been ever since they had entered the mountains.

'I'd like to thank you,' she said, 'for what you have done for us.'

Krob returned her smile, though without any show of friendliness.

'I think you mock me, Marna,' he said quietly, a faint suggestion of threat in his voice. 'You, especially, have little to thank me for.'

'Ah, there I must contradict you,' Marna replied. 'You gave us a guide up the perilous slopes of the mountain; and since our arrival you have fed us and given us shelter.'

'These things are nothing,' Krob said coldly, 'as you well know.'

'Again I must disagree,' Marna answered. 'In my old age I have come to value the simple pleasures. Hot food, a warm bed, good companionship - these cannot be dismissed as nothing. Even you, Krob, must have some experience of them. The love of an old man, for instance, isn't that worth having?'

All at once, like a painted mask being unexpectedly removed, the impression of youth and innocence vanished from Krob's face. The bruised skin around his eyes darkened visibly and he leaned heavily on the Staff whose faint glow flickered and went out.

'You will not speak of such things here,' he said threateningly.

'What things?' Marna said, acting surprised. 'I merely mentioned an old man . . .' She paused meaningfully. 'Oh, I see, you're thinking of Obin, of course. How foolish of me to speak of old men in front of you. But then, it's some time since he died and I'd forgotten how you once loved him. That is right, isn't it, Krob? You did love Obin?'

The area around Krob's eyes grew even darker, more like fire-shrivelled parchment than human skin.

'I've told you . . .' he began.

But Marna, pressing her advantage, interrupted him:

'Yes, you're right, as always. There's no point in recalling those we once knew and loved. Especially when those memories are burdened by guilt and regret.'

All semblance of freshness and youth had left Krob. He stood before her like a worn-out old man, bent forward, swaying slightly, a stick of gnarled and blackened wood clutched in his hand.

'I have no cause for regret,' he faltered out.

'Ah, Krob,' Marna murmured sadly, 'I cannot believe that.' And she pointed at Craak who still crouched at the golden point of the star: 'Why, even that bird continues to feel the pangs of grief. Are you saying you have less heart than that poor dumb creature?'

Krob, his eyes like blank, unseeing cavities, continued to sway from side to side, as though disturbed by some restless wind from the past.

'The bird is of no account,' he said, his voice faint and hesitant.

'Of no account?' Marna said sharply. 'Now it is you who mock me, Krob. Look at it! It stands in Obin's place, at the tenth point of the star. It alone resists your power. And do you know why? Because it reminds you of the past, of an error that can never be wiped out. The greatest of all your crimes, Krob - the foul murder of Obin!'

'He was an old man,' Krob protested feebly.

'Yes, but not old as you are; not consumed by the power of the Staff. He was master of that power; whereas you have allowed it to master you. That is why, when you destroyed Obin, you also destroyed yourself.'

'But he stood in my way,' Krob whispered.

'That at least is true, for he could perceive the danger of the road you had chosen. He tried to deflect you from that road by offering you love and wisdom. Had you allowed him to, he would have been like a father to you. A father, Krob, to you, an outcast since birth. And for that you repaid him with death!'

She paused briefly, and the only sound was the evening wind gently rustling the tops of the trees.

'Was it worth it, Krob?' she asked softly. 'Obin's love, for this? This barren place in which you stand alone? You, an old man before your time, blind and friendless?'

Her voice had grown as gentle as the evening breeze, almost caressing, without hint of accusation. And Derin, watching from outside the Circle, realized that she was making a last appeal, attempting to recall Krob from some distant place in which he wandered alone and lost. Momentarily Krob seemed to harken to that appeal. He raised his face, his eyes now blackened hollows, and turned yearningly towards the sound of her voice.

'All is not lost yet,' she assured him quietly.

For a moment longer he neither moved nor spoke. Then, with a convulsive movement, his hand tightened on the Staff. Gradually the wood began to glow once again, growing steadily brighter until soon it was a sliver of burning white light. And as the Staff gained in brightness, so the burden of age left him. His back became straight, the blackness around his eyes disappeared, and his face grew youthful and fresh.

'This is not the way, Krob,' Marna warned him.

But with a beguiling smile he pointed the glowing Staff towards her, and instantly she staggered and fell, her face ashen and ill, her lips twitching ineffectually as she struggled to speak.

Derin would have leaped to her aid, but he found that he couldn't move, the power which had stricken Marna standing like a wall between them.

He watched as, with a deliberate movement, Krob lowered the Staff.

'Come, Marna,' he said mockingly, 'you aren't defeated so easily, not you, the Witch of Sone. Weren't you also rejected by Obin as I was, and sent homeless, but not empty-handed, from his cave? We understand each other, Marna. I know that such a one doesn't give in after the first encounter.'

She rose painfully to her knees, eyes closed, panting for breath.

'Just one more effort, Marna, that's all you need,' Krob said in the same sarcastic tone. 'Don't throw away those days you've spent journeying here. Get up and do what you must. Show us what you came here for - the real purpose behind all your tricks and lies.'

With her hand on one knee, she levered herself upright and turned to Derin. He had never seen her look so tired and he reached out to support her as she stumbled towards him. But instead of accepting his help, she snatched at the crutch, tearing it from his grasp; and when he tried to retrieve it, she pushed at him with such force that he staggered back against the staircase. Before he could regain his balance she had re-entered the Grove. Yet now she no longer looked feeble and ill: there was an aggressive spring in her step; and the simple wooden crutch which had borne him from the uplands had changed in her hands into a gently glowing staff. At the sight of that transformation, Derin's suspicions of the morning came flooding back, and in an instant he understood at least partly their reason for being in this place.

Powerless to intervene, he stood and watched as Marna circled slowly around the still-smiling Krob. It was not difficult to see why he was so relaxed: the ancient Staff which he held continued to burn with a light so brilliant that it hurt the eyes, far outshining the staff with which Marna threatened him. The outcome, as Derin realized, was inevitable.

'No, Marna,' he shouted, 'don't!'

But ignoring his appeal, she let out a screech of passion and leaped directly at her enemy, the staff whirling in her hands. The very fury of her attack might have daunted a lesser person; but it had no effect on Krob. With an almost casual gesture he raised his own Staff, and immediately the crutch flew from Marna's hands, landing just beyond the Circle, and Marna herself lurched forward and fell at his feet.

In the silence which followed, nobody moved - not Derin, nor Craak, nor the Circle of unseeing old people - and all that could be heard, far louder than the wind, was Marna's hoarse panting as she fought for breath.

Hesitantly, Derin stepped through the gap between two trees.

'Let me help her,' he pleaded.

Krob turned towards him and held up his hand, clearly asking him to wait. In the rapidly fading twilight the burning glow from his Staff was sufficient to illuminate the whole of the Grove, and Derin found himself staring deeply into those strangely bruised eyes.

'First let me tell you the truth which has been withheld from you for so long,' Krob said slowly, 'then we shall see whether you wish to help this old woman.'

'What truth is that?' Derin asked.

Krob laughed quietly to himself, a hollow sound which reminded Derin of the ghostly voices of the bowmen.

'That is an understandable question from one who has been told so many lies,' he said. 'Therefore I shall start at the beginning. You are not the son of an upland farmer, as Marna claims. You come from the woodlands and, like me, are an orphan, an outcast without family or friends. That is why she chose you. You were dispensable, a useful tool in her hands. For consider her purpose: not only did she wish to come here and challenge me; she also sought to smuggle into my presence that puny staff, originally stolen from Obin, with which she hoped to catch me by surprise and so break my power. And how better to accomplish that purpose than by the method she chose?'

'What was that method?' Derin said quietly.

'Need you really ask?' Krob said. 'But yes, after all the lies I suppose you want to be sure. Well then, she began by taking a boy, unwanted and uncared for by anybody, and blotting out his memory of the past. In addition, she bewitched him into thinking he was lame, whereas in fact he was sound of limb. Then, when she had him at her mercy, she told him a series of lies. How that staff of hers was a crutch which the boy had always used; and how his supposed father, that fool called Ardelan whom she persuaded to help her, had been forcibly taken by the soldiers of the Citadel. Oh, and there was one other thing: she filled the boy with shame by persuading him he was selfish and cowardly. In that way she ensured that he would want to follow his father to Iri-Nan - for what boy would not wish to make amends for some cowardly action in the past?'

'But why Iri-Nan?' Derin asked.

'Because she knew that as Witch People you would be under suspicion there, with only one direction open to you - the road here, to the mountains.'

Krob paused for several seconds, giving Derin time to grasp the full significance of all that he had told him.

'So you see,' he went on, 'this old witch has used you. To her you were nothing - a convenience - your lost memory a device to hide the truth from me; your lameness a means of smuggling her staff into the Grove. But I guessed her plan when I saw the bird on your shoulder, for I knew it was attracted not to you, but to the power in the stick you carried.'

Derin passed a hand across his forehead. It was a movement which suggested sadness as much as bewilderment.

'All this I understand,' he said. 'Yet there's one thing missing from your explanation, and that's her reason for using me in this way.'

'That too I thought you might have guessed,' Krob answered patiently. 'Or are you perhaps clinging to the hope that she had the good of others at heart? Because if so, I must disappoint you. You see, many years ago she also went to Obin and asked to be taught by him. But Obin gave her the same answer he first gave me: he told her she was too violent, proud, and ambitious to pursue the path of true knowledge; and he turned her away, knowing she desired only one thing - the Warden's Staff which I now hold. All her life she has dreamed of possessing it, having to make do with that stolen stick of hers. Only in her old age, with the years slipping away from her, did she finally resolve to put her dream to the test. That is why she is here now and why she has used you so ruthlessly: because she yearns to wrest the Staff from me. She cares nothing for wars and the sufferings of those about her – you have heard her admit as much yourself. Her sole concern is to stand supreme within the Grove.'

He stopped once again, and although Derin wanted to argue with him he could think of nothing to say. There was an unnerving thread of logic running through Krob's speech which he could neither deny nor resist.

'Why do you tell me all this?' he said desperately.

'Because we have much in common, you and I: both of us orphans, outcasts, without kin, always being used and rejected by others. That was my initial reason for sparing you. But since then you have done me a service.' Here he pointed to the sword embedded in the block of crystal. 'You put within my reach the Sword of the Kings, the one threat to my power. You even warned me of its true identity, something I might never have guessed. It would now take a witch's staff to free it from its bed of crystal, and such a thing is not likely to happen while I rule here within the Circle. You have therefore made me secure at last, and for that I intend to reward you with your life and freedom. You alone, of all the many people in this domain, may walk at liberty.'

Derin backed away through the trees.

'You tell me that now,' he said, 'but how can I trust you? How can I be sure that any of these things you've said are true?'

'I will give you a token of my good faith,' Krob answered. 'Marna bewitched you into thinking you were lame. I now remove her spell and make you whole again.'

He raised the shimmering Staff and pointed it at Derin's right leg. Immediately he felt a tingling sensation in his ankle. Cautiously he took a single step, half expecting the ankle to give way beneath him; but to his joy his right leg bore the weight. It was true what Krob had said: there was nothing wrong with him. The many days and countless miles he had spent leaning on the crutch had been unnecessary, merely the result of Marna's foolish plan to usurp the power of the Grove. Her curse alone had rendered him lame.

At the thought of the anxiety and discomfort she had forced him to endure, a surge of resentment swept over Derin and he turned angrily towards her. Yet what he saw stilled his rage at once: for there before him was not the cunning and ruthless witch who had used him to achieve her own ends, but rather a tired old woman lying sprawled out on the marble Circle in an attitude of defeat, her thin worn-out body covered by a ragged cloak hardly fit for a beggar. In spite of his lingering resentment he couldn't help feeling sorry for her. And as pity crept into his heart, so certain words she had spoken to him earlier that day came back to him: 'Only a warm and trusting heart can protect us now. Therefore to the heart within you I say: remain watchful and at the ready.' And a little later: 'The heart, Derin, the one place to which Krob cannot penetrate. A place of warmth and love he is too blind to see.' As these words echoed in his mind, he realized they had been a kind of warning – a warning for him to remain on his guard against Krob: Krob the unfeeling one, the master of all reasons, deaf to the promptings of his own heart.

For an instant, recalling Marna's advice, Derin found himself doubting everything Krob had said. And in that instant of doubt, his mind momentarily free of Krob's persuasive logic, he remembered one other thing: a scene in Iri-Nan, when Ardelan had deliberately stamped the ancient emblem of the Citadel on the sand-strewn floor and so proclaimed himself the tenth and secret member of the Council. There, at least, was something Krob had no knowledge of, a small but vital detail which made nonsense of his claim that Marna sought to increase her own power and to rule over the Grove in his place. For how could that possibly be so if she were in league with a member of the Council? No, the very fact that she and Ardelan had conspired suggested that they hoped to achieve some greater and more noble purpose: nothing less than to prevent Krob from plunging the land back into the days of the old Kingdom, a time when the lives and hearts of the people were subject to the cruel whims and fancies of a single man. It was not envy of Krob which motivated Marna, therefore: rather, she sought to destroy the power of the Staff itself.

These thoughts passed so quickly through Derin's mind that Krob suspected nothing. He saw only that Derin had turned resentfully towards the old woman lying at his feet.

'What would you have me do with her?' he said, a cold smile curling his lips.

Derin made a great show of frowning angrily.

'She has much to answer for,' he said. 'I should like you to deliver her to me, so that I can take my revenge in my own way.'

Krob nodded his approval.

'I'm glad to see I haven't misjudged you,' he said. 'Very well, she is yours. But not yet, not until I've broken her spirit and made her like one of these' - he indicated the elders of the Circle who continued to stare before them with unseeing eyes. 'Leave her with me for the remainder of the night,' he added, 'and return at dawn. You may then take what revenge you please.'

There was a harshness in his voice which made Derin tremble for Marna's safety.

'Couldn't I first . . . ?' he began, groping for words.

But Krob cut him short.

'I have made my decision,' he said. 'She is yours at dawn.'

He made an abrupt movement with the Staff, indicating that their conference was over, and Derin, dreading what he might see if he remained, turned and hurried away up the stairs.

Once clear of the Grove and the brightly glowing Staff, he was surprised to find how dark it had become. The tinge of blue in the western sky was rapidly fading, and overhead the cold clusters of stars shone down upon him pitilessly. Never had he felt more helpless and alone. Everything, it seemed, spoke to him of Krob's overwhelming power - the brittle coldness of the air, the sightless figure of Arith standing at the top of the stairs, even the unyielding rocks beneath his feet. Within this desolate place there was nothing and nobody to whom he could turn for help.

Hunching his shoulders against the cold, he trudged wearily across the plateau to the house. In the open doorway he paused briefly and listened: but not a sound, not so much as the rustle of a mouse, greeted him. Dejected, he made his way to the room he had left less than an hour earlier and lay down. He knew the best thing he could do was sleep, but the mere idea of what was happening down in the Grove kept him wide awake. He thought: if only the morning would come; then I could take her away from this place forever. He pictured himself leading Marna out of the Grove and down the mountainside towards the green glades of the woodlands. Yet in his heart he knew that was only a dream. Krob was not so trusting that he would allow Derin to take Marna away: he would want to see the revenge enacted before him. And if Derin desired no revenge? If it became clear that he wished only to rescue Marna? What then?

He closed his eyes, racking his brains in an effort to think of some plan, some means of tricking Krob and saving Marna. Was it possible to devise such a plan? How could anyone resist the power of the Staff? Marna herself had been helpless before it, so who was he to try and outwit Krob?

As the minutes slowly lengthened into hours, he kept being drawn back to a single consideration: to the fact that while Krob held the Staff he was indomitable. Hadn't Marna said as much? And hadn't a whole army of men and women already fallen under his sway? Yet if Krob were really as powerful as he seemed, why had Marna come here and challenged him? What was the point? It made no sense. After all, if there were nothing that could stand against him ... if there were nothing ... if ...

Derin sat bolt upright on the bed and stared through the window at the night sky. When he had stumbled up the stairs from the Grove, those same stars had appeared cold and pitiless; now they looked entirely different, like tiny beacons of light and hope beckoning invitingly to him through the great expanse of blackness.

Springing to his feet, he spent the remaining hours of the night walking restlessly to and fro. By the time the first streaks of grey were showing in the sky overhead, he had decided what had to be done.

Leaving the house, he hurried across the plateau, past the still figure of Arith, and down the stairs. Even without the Staff there would have been enough natural light to guide him, and he saw at a glance that almost nothing had changed since the previous evening. The nine elders continued to stand at the points of the star; the Sword of the Kings remained locked within its crystal prison; Marna's discarded staff lay between the trees where it had been thrown; Craak, more like a smudge of shadow, crouched at the tenth point of the star; and Krob himself stood at the centre of his domain, his Staff shimmering in the early dawn. Only one thing was altered - Marna herself. She was no longer sprawled out on the marble slab. Instead, she was kneeling before Krob, her head lifted towards him, her whole body unnaturally still.

'What have you done to her?' Derin asked, having to struggle to keep the anxiety from his voice.

'See for yourself,' Krob said triumphantly.

He moved the Staff and Marna rose to her feet and turned towards Derin. 'Can you not see the difference?' Krob said. 'The Marna that you knew no longer exists. Only her body remains. Her mind and spirit have been totally dominated by the Staff.'

Derin stared into her eyes, horrified by the blank gaze that met his. For a moment he wondered whether all his thinking and planning had been in vain. But then, somewhere within the depths of those eyes he had once known so well, he saw something stir – not this time the secret presence of Krob gazing furtively out at him, but Marna herself, still surviving, signalling to him her hidden existence, telling him that Krob's victory was not complete.

'Yes, I can see the difference,' Derin said in level tones. 'It is as you say. But even this empty shell is sufficient for my purpose.'

'Before I give her to you,' Krob said, 'I must know what that purpose is. For I will hear no talk of mercy.'

'No more will I!' Derin answered. 'I seek revenge, but of a kind that fits the crime. I wish to strike her down with the very staff with which she burdened me.'

Krob nodded and smiled, showing small pointed teeth.

'I grant your request,' he said.

With unhurried steps, Derin crossed the Circle, walking past the Sword set in its sheath of crystal to the far side of the Grove where the staff lay in the dust between the trees. Stooping, he retrieved the familiar length of smooth wood and weighed it thoughtfully in his hands. Then he turned and walked straight back across the Circle towards Marna. But before he reached her, he suddenly darted sideways and, swinging the staff with all his strength, brought the heavy metal tip crashing down onto the glittering piece of crystal. The clear polished surface, protected by Krob's spell, would have resisted such a blow from any ordinary weapon; but under the impact of the staff it shattered into a thousand gleaming fragments, and with a sharp ring of metal on stone the Sword fell free. No sooner had it touched the marble slab than Derin snatched it up, jerking the blade from its scabbard and turning to face Krob.

For the second time he saw those bruised eyes darken as a shadow of fear passed swiftly across Krob's face.

'There is no need for this,' he said in a dry, choked whisper. 'You will destroy us both!'

'Whatever else happens,' Derin replied, 'I shall at least destroy the Staff. Didn't you realize that is what we came here to do?'

'No, that was only Marna's purpose,' Krob protested, 'not yours. I looked into your mind and I saw no prophecy of this.'

In spite of the tenseness of the situation, Derin found himself smiling - for he was again recalling Marna's words to him on the previous day.

'That was your mistake, Krob,' he said. 'You searched only my mind. Had you looked elsewhere, into my heart for example, you would have seen this possibility clearly enough.'

'You speak in riddles ...' Krob began.

But Derin didn't wait for him to finish. With the Sword held high, he leaped across the Circle. Involuntarily, Krob stepped back and raised the shining Staff. It was merely a defensive action, but it was all that was needed. Before Derin could strike a blow, he felt the Sword shatter in his hand, and he himself was hurled backwards. Had it not been for the trees, he might have sailed out into space and perished on the slopes below. As it was, he slammed into one of the gnarled trunks and fell forward onto his hands and knees. For a time he was too badly winded to move. Yet despite his dizziness and nausea, he realized what had happened. Somehow he had been tricked - by whom he had no idea - but one thing was sure: the sword in the crystal hadn't been the Sword of the Kings and he was again at Krob's mercy.

Groggily he rose to his feet. Krob had already regained his position at the centre of the Circle, his mouth set in a cruel smile.

'You have sealed your fate,' he said, and swung the Staff upwards.

Had he chosen to finish Derin there and then, he could have done so easily. But he paused, relishing his advantage, gazing up at the mountain peaks now visible in the growing light of dawn as though beseeching them to bear witness to his victory. It was a critical and costly delay: because it was then that Craak unfolded his heavy wings and took off. With a loud cry he flew straight at Krob, his black beak thrust forward viciously. Before he could actually close with his enemy, Krob had again sheltered behind the Staff; and repulsed by its enormous power, Craak was sent spinning off into space, his great wings flapping wildly as he fought to resist the invisible forces that buffeted him. Yet his intervention had served its purpose. He had given Derin time to regain his breath and his composure.

Standing now at the very edge of the Circle, Derin knew there was no hope left. A plea for mercy would have been wasted breath. A single course remained open to him: to sell his life as dearly as possible and so force Krob to act violently. In that way he could at least avoid the lingering existence, closer to death than life, which afflicted all who fell under Krob's sway. With this single purpose in mind, Derin groped for the dagger he wore and drew it from its scabbard.

'Only one of us will greet the sun this morning, Krob,' he said.

The threat was more to buoy up his resolve than anything else and he expected Krob to laugh at him. But to his amazement a look of horror swept over Krob's face, the bruised quality about his eyes intensifying until the skin was almost black.

'I did not see it in your mind!' he gasped out. 'I looked, but it wasn't there!'

Bewildered, and at the same time suspicious in case he was being tricked yet again, Derin thrust the flimsy dagger out in front of him, ready to ward off any sudden attack. And only then did he see what had terrified Krob. The small, apparently useless weapon which he had picked up in the snow and carried so far was no longer rusty and battered, its blade hacked and blunt: instead, it shone with a faint glow which grew steadily into a brilliant, unnatural light which matched the radiance of the Staff; and there, inscribed as with fire on the shining metal, was the ancient emblem of the Citadel – a circle of stars within which glowed the ruby outline of a sword.

Close beside him, he heard Marna chuckle softly. It was like a signal to him. Immediately all his resentment and suspicion fell away and he understood everything: the reason for their arduous journey; the necessity for the elaborate web of lies and half-truths which Marna had spun so skilfully; the secret purpose which had persuaded her to blot out his memory of the past – her sole intention not to use or bewilder him, as he had feared, but rather to protect them both from the watchful, probing eyes of Krob. The whole complicated plan, with its many bluffs and evasions, was clear to him at last. Equally important, he finally understood Marna herself: wily old witch who had twisted and turned, plotted and schemed, her every effort directed towards this one moment. The smuggled staff, his own apparent lameness, the sword found in the attic, all nothing more than her means of lulling Krob into a false sense of security, of convincing him that he could see through her plans and ambitions. While all the time she had been outmanoeuvring him, waiting for this single instant of confrontation.

Marna chuckled softly once again, as though prompting him, and Derin moved within the compass of the Circle.

'It is the Sword against the Staff, Krob,' he said quietly, 'as in the old times.'

Krob backed away, leaving the centre of the star vacant.

'You don't know what you're saying!' he protested, his voice high and shrill with desperation. 'You will destroy the Grove, everything! Neither of us will emerge from this alive!'

'There you are wrong, Krob,' Marna answered him. 'Only you will die. The boy has not shackled his soul to the Sword and need not perish with it. He has carried it for weeks and never once guessed its identity. He has even used it without arousing its hidden power. But you! You have allowed your very being to be devoured by the Staff. You cannot exist without it. So lost are you that you cannot see except by its light. It is your eyes, your ears, your youth, your very life itself, and when the light of the Staff is quenched forever, you will dwindle into nothing.'

'No!' Krob cried hysterically. 'This is just another of your tricks!'

But despite his protest, the expression of horror on his face revealed how completely he feared that Marna's judgement might be true. As he struggled with that fear, so the light of the Staff dimmed slightly. It was what Derin had been waiting for. Striding across the Circle, he struck downwards with the shimmering blade of the Sword, aiming not this time at Krob, but at the twisted spiral of light in his hands.

He never felt the actual shock of the impact. As Sword and Staff met, there was a blinding flash, like a bolt of lightning, and a searing pain convulsed Derin's hand and shot up his arm. He staggered aside, his injured hand drawn protectively against his chest.

'Marna!' he called out desperately.

For momentarily he was blinded by the violence of the flash. He felt her arms close about him and, reassured, he turned back towards the Circle. As his sight cleared, he saw that the Sword and Staff had ceased to exist: strewn about the golden star were charred pieces of metal and wood, all that remained of them. And there, in the midst of all the debris, stood the being who had once been Krob. His youthful appearance had left him. In place of the confident young man there was an old bent figure - far too old to be recognizably human: his hands and fingers so crooked and bent that they were more like the dry, twisted twigs and branches of the surrounding trees; his body shattered and deformed by a weight of years too great even to imagine, the crumbling limbs more weathered and eroded than the ancient boulders on the mountainside. But it was his face more than anything else which dismayed Derin: the mouth a sunken toothless hole; his few remaining tufts of hair like withered clumps of discoloured fungus; and what had once been his eyes mere blackened spaces, lightless caverns in which no trace of sight survived.

'What's happened to him?' Derin said in a shocked whisper.

'He is no longer Krob,' Marna answered quietly. 'He gave himself wholly to the Staff, taking on not only its power, but also its great age.'

'Yes, but why has he become like this?' Derin asked.

'With the Staff destroyed and unable to sustain him, he is left only with the burden of its years. He is the last pitiful remnant of its existence.'

As they stood together, watching, the light grew steadily brighter, until at last the top edge of the sun showed itself above the mountain peaks. At the first touch of its warm rays, the thing that had called itself Krob let out a choked and muffled cry and turned its broken face away. With uncertain, trembling steps, it tottered across the marble slab as though trying to escape from the terrible and revealing light of day. At the outer limits of the Circle, it groped towards the trees with its dried, twig-like fingers and, finding a space between them, shambled towards the very edge of the precipice.

'Stop him!' Derin cried, and darted forward.

But the poor, deformed creature had disappeared long before he could reach the edge. And when he looked down, all he could see, far below him on the barren hillside, was a small black stain – the kind of mark left when a piece of seasoned wood is burned until it crumbles into ash.

'He's gone!' Derin said.

'Yes, child, he's gone,' Marna answered.

He turned back to the Grove and saw her standing within the Circle, her face old and sick with weariness, but smiling at him – while all around her the elders of the Circle, their faces suddenly alive once again, blinked and stared at each other in surprise. Nor was that all: slowly descending the stairs was the tall figure of Arith, his eyes no longer dead and unseeing.

'They've all come back!' Derin burst out.

And just as though his words had been a summons, there was a familiar beat of wings above his head and Craak, his feathers ruffled and bent, landed lightly on his shoulder.

14. Bearer of the Staff

For days people streamed away from the mountains, making for their homes in the woodlands, the uplands, or on the plains. Most of them looked shamefaced and confused, but all had lost that dull, lustreless expression imposed on them by Krob. Among the last to leave were Marna and Derin. On a warm evening in early summer they could be seen walking along a path through the lower foothills: Marna, as always, dressed in her ragged cloak, her grey hair more wild and bushy than ever; Derin with Craak on his shoulder and still holding the staff - not now because he needed it to lean on, but because Marna complained that she was too old and tired to carry it.

Just before the sun dipped towards the horizon, they stopped close to a gully from which Derin collected enough wood for a small fire; and as darkness crept over the hillside and the stars appeared one by one in the cloudless sky, they sat together in the warm light of the flames, eating a simple meal of oatcakes. After all the activity at the Grove, it was the first time they had been alone together for some days.

'Well,' Marna said with an obvious sense of relief, 'it's over.'

Derin looked at her ravaged face, still fierce, but oddly calm at last.

'I think what amazes me most,' he said, 'is the way you managed to plan everything as you did.'

Marna smiled, tiny flames reflected in her deep-set eyes.

'There wasn't really as much planning as you might think,' she said. 'Ardelan, as the secret member of the Council, was the keeper of the Sword - he was the one who left it behind for you to find. My main job was to get you to Iri-Nan. For the rest, I had to rely largely on Krob's suspicious nature. I knew he would watch us, and I just hoped he would come to the wrong conclusion - which he did. You see, he judged the world in terms of his own selfish needs, and when he discovered I had bewitched you and tricked you into carrying the staff, he could think of only one thing; that I was plotting to steal his power for myself. That's what he would have done in my position and so he couldn't imagine anything else. Krob really brought about his own downfall.'

'Then you didn't arrange all those other details?' Derin asked. 'The imprint of Ardelan's spear, for instance - which he left in the snow and later in the sand on the floor of our prison cell?'

Marna laughed quietly to herself.

'Oh, those,' she said. 'Yes, they're things I arranged. I suppose you could call them tiny clues. I guessed that if we ever reached the Grove, Krob would accuse me of wanting to steal the Staff for myself. And somehow I had to prove to you that wasn't true. The trouble is, if I'd told you as much, Krob himself would have found out when he probed your mind. So I had to have Ardelan leave you small clues in the hope that you'd spot them. It was a gamble really, but one which paid off. Because you did notice them, and eventually, when it really mattered, they told you what I wanted you to know: that I was in league with the tenth member of the Council and that my purpose was therefore very different from Krob's.'

Derin nodded thoughtfully.

'That explains a lot,' he said. 'With so much uncertainty to worry you, it's no wonder you were often in a bad mood.'

Marna broke into a loud cackle of merriment.

'I've never been famed for my good temper,' she said, 'though it's true that my moods weren't improved by all the things I had on my mind. My chief concern was how to get you to the mountains, and for that part of the journey I had to rely on your independence and good sense. I'm glad to say you didn't let me down. Surely you noticed how cheerful I became once we entered the foothills. I knew then that Krob's curiosity would do the rest for me.'

'Did you also rely on Krob over the business of the false sword?'

'Yes, I enjoyed that,' Marna said, a sly gleam in her eye. 'It wasn't part of the original plan, but when you found the sword in the attic I saw at once that it was too good an opportunity to miss. You'll remember that I didn't actually say it was the Sword of the Kings.'

'But you led me to believe it was,' Derin said.

'Ah yes. I thought to myself, let Krob snatch at our unspoken fears. He was a creature who fed upon fear; and there was no better way of tricking him than by allowing him to observe your anxiety about the sword. To him, that anxiety was the strongest proof of its identity. And with Krob assured that he had discovered the Sword of the Kings, there was a far greater chance of smuggling the true Sword into his presence.'

'That's the one thing which still puzzles me,' Derin said. 'Why didn't he realize it wasn't the true Sword?'

'Because, my child,' Marna explained patiently, 'Krob was a man of extravagant vision. As I said up there on the plateau, he knew nothing of the simple things. It never crossed his mind that the Sword of power might be small and worn and far from beautiful. When he saw the old sword in the attic with its fine workmanship, he immediately trusted your fear and took it for the thing he sought. It fitted his expectations, you see, and for him that was enough. Foolishly, he forgot something every Witch Person is taught: that there is no greater darkness than the blindness of desire.'

They said nothing further that night, both of them curling up beside the fire, secure in the knowledge that they no longer had anything to fear.

When dawn broke, Derin was the first to wake. While Marna was still yawning and stretching, he walked to the edge of the gully and stared out over the plains to the woodlands in the distance.

'What's troubling you, child?' Marna asked him.

He came back to where she was sitting.

'I was wondering where I should go from here,' he said.

'Why, wherever you please,' she said.

He frowned slightly.

'But I have no home,' he said, 'nowhere I can call my own. Even in the woodlands, where I come from, there is no one waiting for me.'

'Is that all that's worrying you?' she replied, giving him a peculiar look. 'In that case, stay with me a while. Accompany me to Ardelan's farm in the uplands.'

'You're going to the uplands?' he said, surprised. 'I thought you'd be returning to Obin's cave.'

'What are you talking about?' she said. 'Why on earth should I go there?'

He squatted in front of her and touched her hands lightly.

'You don't have to pretend with me,' he said quietly, 'because I know who you are. I almost guessed when we first reached the plateau and I saw the emblem of the Circle painted above the door of the house. But now I'm sure: you're the tenth member of the Circle - isn't that so?'

But once again Marna broke into a loud cackle of laughter. For several minutes she couldn't speak, rocking herself from side to side, the tears rolling down her furrowed cheeks.

'Good gracious me!' she said at last, wiping her eyes on the ragged hem of her cloak. 'What nonsense you talk at times. I'm no more the tenth member of the Circle than that mountain peak behind us - though once I had ambitions of that kind. Didn't you hear what Krob said about me? Well, some of it was true. Obin eventually turned me away from the cave - for which I repaid him by stealing the staff you now carry. He said, quite rightly, I was too violent and ambitious and that my task in life was to learn humility by working amongst the people of the uplands. For me that was a difficult task, which I fought against for some years, cherishing that staff like a foolish dream; but I've come to accept that it's the only task I'm fit for. It's perhaps all I deserve: after all I was a thief, like Krob. This journey has been a penance for me, and now I'm the Witch of Sone, nothing more.'

'Then who . . .?' Derin began.

But Marna put her arm affectionately around his shoulders.

'You've questioned and puzzled over things enough for the time being,' she said. 'The best thing you can do now is come with me to the uplands. Ardelan will be waiting for us, and it's as well that we three conspirators have a final meeting before we part.'

Derin agreed and they again set off, keeping to the foothills and striking inland only when they were well to the north.

The uplands, now that summer had come, was far less forbidding than it had been. The rolling pastures were bright green with young grass; and with the farming folk returned from the mountains and the plains, Derin and Marna found they couldn't walk very far without being hailed cheerily by people working in the fields. A dozen times a day they were invited to stop at farmhouses for food and drink; but always they declined gratefully, intent now on reaching their destination and resting from their travels.

Yet when they did eventually get to the burned-out farmhouse, there was little rest to be had. Ardelan had arrived ahead of them and was already felling trees in the wood in order to rebuild the cottage. He stopped working the moment he saw them, his normally serious face wreathed in smiles at the pleasure of finding them safe once again. For a whole afternoon and evening they did nothing but talk of their experiences. But the following morning, as soon as it was light, Ardelan resumed his work.

'The summer in the uplands is short,' he said by way of explanation. 'There is much to be done before the cold winds return.'

And Derin, glad of an excuse not to think about the future, went with him to the woods and helped him fell and drag back the heavy logs.

That first day set the pattern for the many that were to follow. Each morning Derin rose at dawn and worked until dusk. Then, after a hearty meal, exhausted by his labours, he slept soundly the night through. In its way, it was a contented kind of existence, all his attention fixed on the immediate task of rebuilding the farmhouse, and later of building a barn in which to shelter Ardelan's newly acquired cattle. Yet at the back of his mind he knew he was merely putting off the moment of decision, that sooner or later he would have to go off somewhere and make a life of his own.

As if sensing his secret thoughts, Craak grew steadily more restless. To begin with, he was content to remain close to Derin; but soon he began flying off alone, sometimes remaining away for hours. And by summer's end, even when he was with Derin he spent most of his time perched high in a tree calling out plaintively, as if he were urging Derin to leave this foreign place and go back to where he truly belonged.

It was Craak's restlessness which finally persuaded him. He awoke one morning and found that a cold wind was blowing. The air was sharp and fresh and smelled of the coming winter; and the trees in the small wood were scattering their few remaining leaves across the pasture. As Derin stepped outside, shivering in the cool wind, Craak flew past him, his great black wings carrying him towards the south.

'Craak,' Derin called out.

With obvious reluctance the bird circled and came back, perching on the ridge of the newly constructed farmhouse.

'Craak,' he called back to Derin.

But there was a dismal quality about his cry which could no longer be ignored. And suddenly Derin knew what had to be done.

Ducking back inside the farmhouse, he collected his few simple belongings and went to Marna and Ardelan who were still eating breakfast.

'Winter will soon be here,' he said. 'It's time for me to be going.'

'Where will you head for?' Ardelan asked him.

'For the woodlands. It's the only home I know.'

Ardelan stood up and took Derin's hand warmly in his.

'We have a great deal to thank you for,' he said quietly.

As soon as he released Derin's hand, Marna, without a word, put both arms about his neck and kissed him on the forehead and cheeks.

'Go well, my child,' she whispered gently.

Derin turned and stumbled towards the door. Before he could open it, Marna called after him:

'Don't forget to take the staff with you.'

He stopped and stared back at her, puzzled.

'Why should I take it?' he said.

'Because it's yours,' she answered simply. 'Obin is dead, and you are the one who carried it to and from the mountains.'

'But it bears the emblem of the Grove,' he objected. 'Surely it belongs rightfully to the tenth and secret member of the Circle.'

'That is true,' she said, a knowing smile on her old face.

It took him several minutes to grasp the meaning of her words; and even then he didn't answer immediately.

'You mean . . . ?' he began, and stopped, feeling more dazed and bewildered than he ever had during their long journey.

It was Ardelan who came to his rescue.

'Why do you think Craak stays with you?' he said quietly. 'His place is with the master of the cave.'

Still unable to answer, Derin walked over to the window and

gazed out. He was thinking how, months earlier, he had asked himself why he should have been the one chosen by Ardelan. Now, it seemed, he had his answer.

Turning back to the room, he said:

'But I know nothing.'

'That is not true,' Marna corrected him. 'Already you know something I have never learned fully: humility - the knowledge that, in order to lead others, you must first know how to serve them.'

'Even if I accept what you say,' he protested, 'who am I to lead anyone? I have no understanding of the ways of the Witch People.'

'Asti is waiting for you in the cave,' Marna said. 'She realized long ago who you are, as did Craak. She will teach you what you need to know.'

But at this Derin shook his head.

'No,' he said firmly. 'Asti is not much older than I am. She still has much to learn herself. We both need someone who is steeped in the knowledge of the Witch People.'

'And where do you propose to find this teacher?' Marna asked.

'He means you, Marna,' Ardelan said with a smile.

'Me?' she said, almost as surprised as Derin had been a few minutes earlier. 'Didn't I tell you that Obin sent me away and that I was a thief? That I was ordered by the master of the cave to work here in the uplands?'

'Yet now,' Ardelan put in quickly, 'it would seem the master of the cave has told you otherwise. Your duty lies elsewhere, in the woodlands.'

Marna looked steadily at Derin.

'Is this truly what you desire?' she asked him - and then held her hand up before he could speak. 'Don't answer hastily,' she said. 'You know my temper and how impatient I can be; and I warn you now, I would be a hard taskmaster.'

But Derin only grinned at her.

'Even with Asti and Craak to keep me company,' he said, 'life would be dull without you, Marna.'

'Then it is decided,' Ardelan said.

'Oh, I don't know about that,' Marna grumbled. 'After all, it's a long way to the woodlands and I've had more travelling recently than my old bones can bear.'

But despite her many complaints, less than an hour later she and Derin were again journeying across the uplands.

To the casual observer, their present journey would not have appeared very different from their earlier one. Marna remained what she had always been: a fierce old woman dressed in a ragged cloak. And Derin, although a little taller and no longer lame, was still a boy rather than a man. Even the weather was similar, for the day had turned much colder and now sleet was blowing into their faces and covering the surrounding countryside with a thin white layer - a fact which caused Marna to complain bitterly. Yet in spite of these similarities, there was of course a world of difference between the two journeys. That difference was probably best captured by the antics of a large black bird flying high above their heads. He was swooping and diving with carefree abandon, a picture of joy as he frolicked happily in the boisterous wind.

Also by Victor Kelleher

FORBIDDEN PATHS OF THUAL

When the villages of the coast are overrun by the Mollag, the boy Quen is sent out secretly into the ancient and forbidding forest of Thual to get help. But his journey lies far beyond the forest: for, if the quest is to be successful, Quen must find his way into the very presence of the Wise Ones. His survival and that of the community he comes from depend in the end on his own determination and mental discipline.

THE HUNTING OF SHADROTH

The story of a boy despised by his Clan, but who has an extraordinary gift that can save them from disaster. Since time immemorial the people of the Clan have lived peacefully on the Slopes overlooking the Greenlands. But then a powerful and mysterious evil threatens to overwhelm them, and the survival of the Clan depends on the success of Tal's perilous journey to find help.

Some other Puffins

THE WORLD AROUND THE CORNER

Maurice Gee

When Caroline discovers an old pair of cracked spectacles in her father's junk shop, she has no idea how important they are. Even when she puts them on and sees things very differently, she doesn't guess that the safety of another world depends on them.

UNDER PLUM LAKE

Lionel Davidson

On the wild cliffs of Cornwall, a young boy finds a path that leads down to a cave – and so begins a journey into a world of marvels. He learns the things he should never have learned – in a fantastic realm under the sea where the people live for hundreds of years. Pain is meaningless to them, and they get their thrills from whizzing down the power slopes of switched-on mountains or sky-diving in kites over aromatic waters. In this beautiful and compelling book, Lionel Davidson stirs half-forgotten memories, dreams and desires in us all.

NOTHING TO BE AFRAID OF

Jan Mark

The characters in Jan Mark's stories are the sort of people who create their own imaginary world of horrors . . . and then get trapped in it because these are the sort of horrors that won't go away. They follow you upstairs in the dark and slide under the bed, and there they stay . . . Meet young William, who has his own version of a well-known tale, irritating Arthur who thinks he knows everything, poor Brenda who's caught between the animosity of two teachers, and a host of other strange and cunning characters.

A RAG, A BONE AND A HANK OF HAIR

Nicholas Fisk

After a terrible nuclear accident the birthrate has dropped dramatically. The only hope appears to lie with the Reborns – new people made chemically by scientists. But the Reborns have been given free will and no one is quite certain how they will behave . . .

THE SHADOW GUESTS

Joan Aiken

The deep mystery surrounding the disappearance of Cosmo's mother and elder brother had never been solved. Then peculiar things began to happen at the old mill house where he was staying. Strangers appeared and only Cosmo could see them; what did they want? Where, or *when*, did they come from?

GHOST IN THE WATER

Edward Chitham

It all started when Teresa and David discovered the curious inscription on a gravestone in the local churchyard: *In Memory of Abigail Parkes. Departed this Life 10th December 1860. Aged 17. Innocent of all Harm.* It was these last words that excited their curiosity, and they determined to find out all about Abigail and solve the mystery of her sudden death. How could they know that the dead girl's life was mysteriously linked to their own?

HEARD ABOUT THE PUFFIN CLUB?

.... it's a way of finding out more about Puffin Books and authors, of winning prizes (in competitions), sharing jokes, a secret code, and perhaps seeing your name in print! When you join you get a copy of our magazine, *Puffinalia*, sent to you four times a year, a badge and a membership book.
For details of subscription and an application form, send a stamped addressed envelope to:

The Australian Puffin Club
Penguin Books Australia Limited
P.O. Box 257
Ringwood
Victoria 3134

and if you live in England, for a copy of *Puffin Post* please write to

The Puffin Club Dept A
Penguin Books Limited
Bath Road
Harmondsworth
Middlesex UB7 ODA